I0549905

TRUST

A HARMLESS WORLD NOVEL

THE WULF FAMILY
BOOK THREE

MELISSA SCHROEDER

EDITED BY
NOELLE VARNER

COVER ART BY
SCOTT CARPENTER

HARMLESS PUBLISHING

For the Harmless World readers.

Also by Melissa Schroeder

The Harmless World

The Original Harmless Five

- A Little Harmless Sex
- A Little Harmless Pleasure
- A Little Harmless Obsession
- A Little Harmless Lie
- A Little Harmless Addiction

Rough 'n Ready

- Rough Submission
- Rough Fascination
- Rough Fantasy
- Rough Ride

Harmless Trouble

- Harmless Secrets
- Harmless Revenge
- Harmless Scandals

The Wulf Family

- Faith
- Taboo
- Trust

A Little Harmless Military Romance

- Infatuation
- Possession
- Surrender

Task Force Hawaii

- Seductive Reasoning
- Hostile Desires
- Constant Craving
- Tangled Passions
- Wicked Temptations
- Twisted Emotions-coming 2025

THE CAMOS AND CUPCAKES WORLD

Camos and Cupcakes

- Delicious
- Luscious
- Scrumptious

The Fillmore Siblings

- Hate to Love You
- Love to Hate You

Juniper Springs

- Wild Love
- Crazy Love
- Last Love
- Imperfect Love

THE SANTINI WORLD

The Santinis

- Leonardo
- Marco
- Gianni
- Vicente
- A Santini Christmas
- A Santini in Love
- Falling for a Santini
- One Night with a Santini
- A Santini Takes the Fall
- A Santini's Heart
- Loving a Santini

Semper Fi Marines

- Tease Me
- Tempt Me
- Touch Me

The Fitzpatricks

- Chances Are
- Only You-*coming in 2025*

THE MELISSA SCHROEDER INSTALOVE COLLECTION

Dominion Rockstar Romance

- Undeniable
- Unpredictable
- Unexpected
- Tempted

Mafia Sisters

- Stealing Destiny
- Guarding Fable

Faking It

- Faking it with my Billionaire Boss
- Faking it with my Brother's Best Friend
- Faking it with my Frenemy

The Fighting Sullivans

- Falling for the General's Daughter
- Falling for the Girl Next Door
- Falling for my Best Friend
- Falling for my Baby Mama

Also Included

- Kiss my Tinsel
- Dad Bod Rockstar

Texas Temptations

- Conquering India
- Delilah's Downfall

Hawaiian Holidays

- Mele Kalikimaka, Baby
- Sex on the Beach
- Getting Lei'd

Once Upon an Accident

- The Accidental Countess
- Lessons in Seduction
- The Spy Who Loved Her

The Cursed Clan

- Callum
- Angus
- Logan
- Fletcher
- Anice

The Sweet Shoppe

- Tempting Prudence
- Cowboy Up
- Her Wicked Warrior

By Blood

- Desire by Blood
- Seduction by Blood

Hands On

- The Hired Hand
- Hands on Training

Telepathic Cravings

- Voices Carry
- Lost in Emotion
- Hard Habit to Break

Bounty Hunters, Inc

- For Love or Honor
- Sinner's Delight

Saints and Sinners

- Seducing the Saint
- Hunting Mila

Lonestar Wolf Pack

- Primal Instincts

Texas Heat

- Scorched

Spies, Lies, and Alibis

- The Boss

Single Titles

- A Calculated Seduction

CONTENTS

Hawaiian Terms

Aloha - Hello, goodbye, love
Bra-Bro
Bruddah- brother, term of endearment
Haole-Newcomer to the islands
Hiwahiwa - precious
Howzit - How is it going?
Kamaʻāina-Local to the islands
Mahalo-Thank you
Malasadas- A Portuguese donut without a hole which started out as a tradition for Shrove (Fat) Tuesday. They are deep fried, dipped in sugar or cinnamon and sugar. In other words, it is a decadent treat every person must try when they go to Hawaii. If you do not try it, you fail. Do yourself a favor. Go to Leonard's and buy one. You are welcome.
Pupule - crazy
Slippahs - slippers, AKA sandals

PROLOGUE

J akob Wulf stood and looked out the floor-to-ceiling windows. The waves at Sunset Beach were a little raucous, and crazy people were out there trying to tame them. Being a Brit, he didn't exactly grow up near good surfing. Still, he came from a traveling family—thanks to the multitude of beaches that spanned the globe, but there was nothing like Hawai'i. He'd only been on the island for two days, but he might be in love.

"Hey," Benedict Kingston broke into his thoughts. "I gotta talk to my uncle about this upcoming invitational, so I'll meet you on the beach."

Ben had agreed to show Jake the ropes about surfing. He had to play a surfer in his next movie, and he wanted to know everything there was to know about the competition and the business.

Thanks to his agent, he was now hooked up with the premiere surfing company on the island. His namesake was his father, who moved to the islands and promptly fell in love with a pretty Hawaiian woman. They'd built Kingston Surfing from the ground up. It was a massive company that was still family-run.

"Okay."

"My sister is down there. She's a good surfer, so ignore how young she is. Also, since she's so young, no hitting on her."

Jakob frowned. He knew he hadn't always had the best reputation when it came to women. The truth was that about eighty percent of the rumors about him were false. But he never played around with underaged women. He might only be twenty-one, but his mother had raised him better than that.

"No worries, bra," he said, which made Ben laugh.

"We need to work on your accent, bra."

Jakob smiled because there was no condemnation in the other man's tone. He knew Ben respected him because Jakob had spent the last day learning as much as he could about the Hawaiian culture surrounding surfing.

"I'll see you in a few minutes," Ben said, smiling as he headed to his meeting.

It only took him about five minutes to get to the beach. Another thing he loved about Hawai'i. You were never that far from the beach. For an Englishman, he had thin blood. He hated London weather. It felt like he never saw the sun there. Here, the sun was almost always shining.

Jakob relished the warm sand as he walked across the beach. He had grown a little facial hair, wore a pair of aviator sunglasses, and had on a Kingston Surfing ball cap. While he didn't always get recognized, he wanted to avoid it as much as possible. He wanted to just enjoy the beach.

That's when he saw her again. It was the woman he had been admiring, and she was still killing it. She was coming in on a massive wave that scared the shit out of him, but she seemed to be part of it. Her feet were steady as she maneuvered the board, her long dark hair flowing behind her.

She was magnificent. If he were poetic, he might say she was the goddess Pele reincarnated. As she made her way to the beach, she grabbed her board and moved in his direction. She wore a wet suit that cut off at the thighs but covered much more than any bikini Jakob had ever seen. Didn't matter. She was stunning. Her golden eyes widened when she saw him, and she headed his way.

"Trying to stay incognito?"

There was just enough sassy humor in her voice that his mouth twitched. "Something like that."

"You don't have to worry much about that today. Lots of surfers out, but they don't give a damn who you are."

He glanced around and realized it was true. It was a relief and a bit freeing. He hadn't realized how tense the paps had made him recently.

"I'm Jakob Wulf."

She grinned at him, her golden eyes twinkling up at him. "Yeah, I know."

He rolled his eyes, glad she couldn't see it behind his mirrored lenses. He didn't get tongue-tied around women, but this woman was insanely beautiful. And she apparently didn't care who he was.

He opened his mouth to get her name and hopefully her number when he heard Ben shout his name. Jake turned in the direction of his voice.

"Here comes trouble," the woman murmured.

Frowning, he glanced at the woman. "You know him?"

"You could say that."

"Sorry about that. Uncle Abe can be a stickler for details."

"No worries," Jakob said.

"You should know better than to get pulled into a meeting with him. He likes the sound of his own voice," the woman said, but she was smiling.

A sinking feeling hit Jakob as he realized who this woman was.

"So, you've met my little sista, Lani?"

Well, fuck.

ONE

Lani Kingston did everything in her power not to show how irritated she was with the interview she had been forced into. The lights were hot. She was sure she was sweating like a baboon in heat, and the host...well, he was annoying.

"So, one last question," Devon Peters said, flashing that million-dollar smile. Lani was surprised that he hadn't blinded her with how white his teeth were. He wore a Hawaiian shirt but didn't look right in it. It was as if he were dressed up for a costume party. She knew he was a haole, or newcomer, to the islands, but she felt as if he looked down on their culture.

"Of course."

It wasn't like she could tell him to get bent. She was on camera, and one thing she would never do as head of PR at Kingston Surfing was cause a scandal.

"With your brother getting married this weekend, there's been speculation about you and Rick Bellows."

She held her smile even as her stomach twisted in knots. Lani knew the question was going to come, and having to deal with speculation about Rick was something she was used to.

However, since her brother started planning his wedding, there had been more speculation on social media about him and Royal.

"Has there been?"

Yep, this guy always treated her like she was an idiot. Fluff reporters like him never stood a chance with her. She might run the PR for their company, but she also had a law degree.

Granted, there was no chance of a wedding—not when he couldn't keep it in his pants. She would never again date someone like Rick. It had been her own fault. He had been asking her out for about nine months when she finally gave in. The reason for that was too embarrassing to think about.

"That's not a no."

That shark smile was getting on her nerves. She'd been dealing with men like him for years. Peters thought he was an apex predator when he wasn't even a beta male.

"Was there a question? I think that was more of a state-ment." He opened his mouth, but she decided to end his stupid speculation. "And besides, this has nothing to do with Kingston Surfing."

"Rick Bellows is your top surfer."

"True. But I didn't ask about your latest date...or should I say scandal."

What little color he had on his face seemed to vanish. That's right. She never went into an interview without some informa-tion about the reporter. Not that everyone on Oahu didn't know that Peters was going through a nasty divorce since he had been caught by his soon-to-be ex-wife with his producer.

"That's not pertinent to the interview."

"And neither is my relationship with Rick. I'm sure you understand about keeping things professional."

The interview lasted for a few minutes as she answered a couple more questions about the invitational, and then they ended it.

Once the cameras were off, Peters' stupid smile vanished. "Not cool, Lani."

She blinked at him. "What? Not wanting to answer questions about my relationship with Rick? It's almost like I'm held to another standard than any man."

He sniffed—actually sniffed—at her. "Your relationship has a lot to do with the company. Your company sponsors him."

"Then ask him about it. Or maybe you would like me to have my brother talk to you."

His eyes widened. "N-no."

Yeah, her brother was a massive threat, but it was just that, a threat. Her brother was too wrapped up in his wedding, and soon-to-be wife to even care what was going on with her. Although, she was sure she would get a call later from him complaining. These days, he never hesitated to blast her for one thing or another. Still, he held much power on the island, especially advertising power. Peters knew that it could sink his already dwindling career.

"Now, I have some things to do for my brother's wedding, if you don't mind."

He nodded, and she headed out of the studio. Maybe she imagined it, but a few women smiled brighter as she passed. Yeah, Peters wasn't well-liked. He had a reputation for being a slobbering drunk who couldn't keep it in his pants.

She slipped on her sunglasses as she exited the Hawai'i Live studios. It was late morning and brighter than when she'd entered the studio. Nothing new for her, but when she realized she was looking for her little red Mustang, not the SUV she had driven in for her errands, she sighed. She hated the company car, but when she'd had issues with her brakes earlier that week, she hadn't had a choice. Thankfully, nothing happened when her brakes failed since she hadn't been driving. It had been in her brother's driveway.

Now, though, it meant she had to drive around in the behemoth of a vehicle. Although, considering her next errand, it was probably a good thing. As she pulled out of the parking lot and hit Ala Moana Street, the muscles in her neck knotted. Why she had to pick up Jake, she had no idea, but her brother had insisted. The guy was a billionaire actor. She was pretty sure he could get himself to the family house. But her brother Ben had insisted.

As she sped up to take the onramp for H-1, she tried to get her nerves to settle. It was bad enough that she was pretty much acting as the contact for this stupid wedding. Now, she was saddled with the most irritating man on the face of the earth.

Most women would trade places with her in a heartbeat. The man was Hollywood gold with an English accent and a devil-may-care attitude that most people found charming. She did not. The two of them always found themselves at odds. And since he was why she had dated Rick in the first place, she was even more annoyed.

Nope. Not today. She would not go down the *Jakob made me do something* trail. She was a big girl who understood her own actions, and it was her fault.

She took the exit for the airport, knowing she didn't have to rush. No, Mr. Jakob Wulf, two-time Oscar nominee and celebrated heartthrob, always flew private. Even though her family had a private plane like the Wulfs, she rarely used it.

After parking, Lani sat in the silence and tried to compose

herself. Dealing with Jakob Wulf took a lot of composure, especially these days. Part of it was his personality. Another part was the embarrassment she still felt for her stupid crush. Thank God that was gone, but she remembered trying to flirt with her brother's friend when she was only sixteen.

He was still considered one of the hottest men around. There were rumors he was going to win that magazine award again. He had it all. Wealth, looks, a great career. But he seemed so dissatisfied with life these days. Jake didn't lash out. That just wasn't his way. Instead, he cracked jokes.

Sighing, she slipped out of her car and headed to the terminal. The late morning sun was already beating down on her. As a Hawaiian, she usually enjoyed the hotter days. Her blood was thin, but just like Jake, she was now dissatisfied with life. Or rather, she was unhappy with the situation her brother was putting her in.

Pushing that thought away, she stepped into the terminal. He wasn't there, of course, but she knew he would be there momentarily. With a sigh, she started to pace around. Lani had never had much patience. It was one of her biggest faults. Of course, it allowed her to graduate from high school a year early, and it only took her three years to get her BA before moving on to law school.

There was a buzz in the terminal, which caught her attention. Of course, whenever Jakob Wulf appeared, there were fans, mainly women. He pretended like he didn't notice. She knew he did because his mouth twitched. And he didn't have to come through the terminal because he had a private flight. He probably did it just because of this reaction.

Tall and golden. It was the way she'd always thought of Jakob. The man never seemed to have a care in the world, even though she knew he had a quick financial mind that helped with the family business. He was already in shorts and a t-shirt, with a ball cap embroidered with the Wulf Resorts logo.

As always, she steeled herself before he reached her. His eyes sparkled.

"Good afternoon, Lani."

Damn, that accent still had her toes curling in her shoes. "It's still morning here."

He nodded, but his mouth tipped up in a smile. "Sorry. Good morning."

She grunted in response, and he grinned. Why he always seemed to be amused by her, she had no idea.

"I take it you have no bags."

He shook his head. "They'll make it to the house."

"Let's go."

He waved a hand. "You lead, and I will follow."

She turned and did just that.

Jakob tried his best not to roll his eyes, but it was difficult. Following Lani was a mistake. The woman was...well, she was perfect.

He loved how her navy-blue pencil skirt hugged her full, heart-shaped ass. And the heels...Jakob rolled his eyes. She was trying to kill him and every other heterosexual male around.

Just that thought had him glancing around at the sparse crowd. He gave more than a few of the men mean looks. He knew it was way out of line, but so was his infatuation for his best friend's little sister. That was the reason he had avoided the island for so long. Even when he went to Maui for Jules' wedding a few months ago, he had made an excuse for not coming to see Ben.

Once they crossed the street and headed into the parking garage, he looked around for Lani's little convertible. She loved that thing, and he had been looking forward to driving with the top down.

She stopped by a behemoth of an SUV. He frowned.

"What happened to your Mustang?"

"Had some problems with the breaks, so I'm driving one of the company's SUVs."

As they settled in the seats, he frowned. "What kind of brake problems?"

"They weren't working."

Alarm rushed through him. "What happened? Did you get hurt?"

She shook her head as she frowned at him. "I noticed the problem before anything happened. And apparently, I'm not hurt. I'm fine."

"Why didn't Ben call me?"

She frowned at him. "Why would he?"

Exactly.

"Besides, he acted like it was no big deal."

"What the hell?"

She snorted as she started up the SUV. "But don't worry. I know how you like the sun."

Lani hit a button, and that's when Jakob noticed the SUV had a sunroof.

He said nothing as they headed out of the parking garage and the airport. The Honolulu Airport wasn't big. Only so many flights could come in daily, so it wasn't the nightmare that

LAX or Heathrow was. It was something he was looking forward to once he moved here.

He'd just signed on to the new show *Task Force Honolulu*. No one but the studio and his people knew about it. The announcement would come in the next two weeks. Well, he had told his family. Jules was thrilled. His mother and his sister-in-law Nicola—not so much. It was weird that within the last few years, he had gained a sister-in-law he adored and a brother-in-law he admired.

"What's that smirk for?" Lani asked as she took the onramp to H-1 West.

"I was thinking about my siblings getting married and how I went from two to four siblings. It's nice. You'll see." She snorted, and his smile faded. "What's that for?"

"What?"

"The snort."

She sighed. "Royal doesn't like me."

"That can't be true."

"It's okay," she said, dismissiveness filling her voice. "I don't like her, so we're even."

"What? Why?"

Her shoulders were hunched in a little. Alarm sped through him. Lani wasn't the type of woman to hunch her shoulders. It was then that he realized she was taking the exit for H-3.

"I thought we were going to go see Ben first?"

"We are," she said.

"Have you moved your headquarters from the North Shore?"

That would have made news. Kingston Surfing had been around for decades. Relocating their headquarters would have sent shockwaves through Hawai'i and the entire surfing world.

"He's not at work. He's at home."

He frowned, and then it hit him. "He took off this week for the wedding. I didn't even think about that."

"He hasn't been working full-time for close to six months."

Then she bit her lip. As if she revealed some big secret. He wouldn't have noticed it if he hadn't been studying her so closely. "What?"

She sighed again. "I don't want to gossip about Ben."

Meaning that there was a whole lot more, but she wouldn't tell him. He would find out sooner or later, but she seemed… fragile. So different from the Lani he knew. She still had that spine of steel, but he felt as if one wrong word and she might start crying. And that was not like Lani at all.

From the time he'd met her, she'd had enough moxie to match his. In fact, he always suspected she had more. But for some reason, she seemed different.

She might not realize it, but he would find out soon enough, either from her or her brother.

"I'm still surprised Ben didn't mention your brake situation." And he would be cornering his best friend about that.

She shrugged. "He's been busy with the wedding stuff."

He was calling bullshit. The guy he knew for a decade just didn't shrug off his sister's brakes going out. This was the guy who had threatened Jakob before he'd even met Lani.

Oh, yeah, they were going to have a chat today about that, and maybe he would discover what had Lani looking so damned sad.

Two

Dread inched down Lani's spine as she parked the car in front of her brother's house. She used to live here. It had long been a family compound their grandparents had built, but once Royal had moved in, Lani hadn't felt welcome. And she hated the other woman for making her avoid Ben. They been close at one time, but in the last year, he had distanced himself from her. Worse, he had been taking advice from Royal, who didn't know squat about running any business, let alone a surfing giant like Kingston Surfing.

"You're sighing more than Jules did when she was a teenager."

She glanced at Jakob. When had he gotten so damned observant? Most of the time, he acted like she didn't exist.

"Royal is...a lot."

"That's a nice way of putting it."

Lani tilted her head. "Have you met her?"

"No. But I've seen her social media."

So, he didn't see how mean she was.

"And I smell mean girl."

She blinked. "You do?"

"No. Not at first. I talked to Nic and Jules about her."

Lani knew that other than his mother, the two women were the most important women in his life. Nic had been his brother's sober companion before stepping into her role as executive assistant for the whole company. She was now also Jensen's wife. Jules was the sweetest woman Lani had ever met, so she understood why Jakob loved his sister so much.

"And?"

"Nic said she heard things. You know how she is. She knows everyone in PR and social media, and she said Royal had a reputation for being rude."

She nodded. Rude wasn't a big thing. "Let's go before Ben comes out here complaining."

Another frown from Jakob. How did he look so crazy hot frowning? Of course, he looked crazy hot doing anything.

She opened her door, but Jakob was already rushing around the front of the vehicle. "Let me help you down."

"What? Why?"

His mouth twitched.

"Stop."

He cocked his head and studied her for a moment. It was an odd situation having him standing there looking up at her.

"Stop what?"

"Laughing at me."

"You think I'm laughing at you?"

"You're always laughing at me."

The moment she said it, she regretted the words. Or, actually, the tone. It sounded so sad, so pathetic. It had been a bad few months. That's all.

"I'm not laughing at you. You just make me happy."

"Say what now?"

His mouth twitched once more. "You don't treat me any different than you treat your brother. It's hard to find people—especially women—who don't try to gain my favor."

"Oh. It must be tough fending off all of the attention."

"And you just proved my point."

He went to take her by the waist, but she stopped him.

"What is with you?"

"What do you mean?"

"Listen, I get that I don't drool over you like other women."

"I should be so lucky. How is Rick, by the way?"

She swallowed her irritation. Or at least, she tried. Jakob could always get on her last nerve.

"I have no idea."

"And why is that? I thought he would be here for the wedding."

Unfortunately, Rick Bellows would be at the wedding as their top surfer. Nothing like seeing your recent ex at your brother's wedding.

"I assume he will be, but that has nothing to do with me."

"Well, his loss."

With that pronouncement, he plucked her off the seat and set her down on the driveway.

"Not sure he sees it that way," she muttered as she tried to step around Jakob, but he stopped her.

"Then he's an idiot. You were the catch in that relationship, and any man who doesn't realize that is an ass."

Warmth filled her even as she warned herself not to get all goo-goo over a man who pretended to be other people for a living.

"Thank you. But I suggest we head inside before Ben storms out here to ask why I'm monopolizing your time."

As if on cue, her brother's voice rang out across the driveway. "What is taking you so long?"

"You *do* know him well."

She used to, but she just nodded. They stepped away from the SUV and shut the door. As Jakob waved for her to proceed him—always with pretty manners—her phone buzzed. When she saw the number, she knew she had to be discreet about this call.

"You go ahead. I have to take this."

He took off his aviators, his gaze roaming over her. She knew he wanted to say something, but her brother opened his stupid mouth again. At least, this time, he was helping her. Jakob nodded, but his expression warned he was going to dig more.

As soon as she was alone, she moved away from the vehicle.

"Where are you going?" Ben called out. Interesting that he seemed to see that she was in the area. Lately, the brother who had always been one of her best friends had not only been ignoring her, but it felt as if aliens had taken over his body. His personality had changed so much in the last year.

"Got a call I have to take from the caterers."

He nodded as if she worked for him. Granted, she worked for Kingston and had planned to take over the entire legal department when Auntie Mae retired, but lately, she had been having second thoughts. Hence the phone call.

She clicked on her phone to answer the call.

"Lani," Conner Dillon said. He owned one of the best-known security companies on the island. They had made a name for themselves since Conner moved to Oahu a few years ago. They were headquartered in Miami, but Hawai'i was uniquely positioned worldwide.

"Conner. How are you doing?"

"Doing well. I wanted to touch base with you about my offer."

Yes, *the offer*. The last few months had been difficult. Her brother had become a stranger, and things at the business seemed off. She and Mae had talked about it, but neither could find anything. Add in her cheating ex, Rick, and she had been through a lot. When Conner had popped up and told her they were looking for someone to handle all their legal issues in the Pacific Rim, she had played with the idea.

"I have been thinking about it."

"Look, I'm not calling to pressure you, especially with everything happening." Everyone on the islands and beyond knew about her brother's upcoming wedding. "I just wanted to let you know the offer still stands. We want someone from the islands to handle the legal issues, and with your background, I think you will fit right in."

She would. She had contacts in surfing, but it went beyond that. She had dealt with sponsors worldwide. Auntie Mae had been training her for years to take over. Lani might be the head of PR, but Mae was adamant that Lani would take her spot.

"Can I have another few days? Ben's wedding is this weekend."

"Yes, I know. I saw your interview."

She sighed.

"That reporter is a dick." She heard a murmur in the background, and she figured it was Conner's wife, Jillian. "Sorry. He was a jerk."

"You were right the first time."

He chuckled. "How about we meet up next Wednesday for lunch? That will give you some time to regroup after the wedding, which I'm sure will be exhausting."

It was. If she ever got married, Lani would only want her family and her groom's family there. Maybe a few close friends.

"That sounds great, Conner."

"I'll text you Tuesday and set up a time."

After signing off with him, she stood there for a long moment, letting the idea of not working for Kingston fill her. It was heartbreaking, in a way. Their family, as had she, had been part of the surfing community for decades. Even when she had gone to the mainland, she had spent her time off in Hawai'i helping out in the legal department.

But something else joined that pain...freedom and excitement. She had never even had a part-time job unless it had something to do with Kingston. Even when she interned, it had been with a subsidiary of their company on the mainland. This would be the first time she'd ever stepped out on her own.

Maybe it was time to do just that.

"You're looking great," Ben said as they settled on the leather sectional. It was buttery soft, and situated so he could see the waves crashing into the beach.

"Thanks."

"I guess working less is good for you."

He noted the comment and filed it away. He couldn't put his finger on it, but something was different about his best friend. It had been months since they had been together.

Dressed in a Hawaiian shirt and shorts, he looked the same as usual. There was something off about him, though.

"Been keeping busy." He had his family business, but he had also stepped into producing. It was one of the things he had always wanted to do. That and direct. One of the reasons he had taken a chance on the new series was that they'd agreed to let him direct one episode of the first season.

"Sure, sure."

"Why didn't you tell me about the brake issue with Lani's car?"

His friend waved Jakob's worry away. "Oh, it's no big deal. She knows how to drive well, so she was safe."

And the alarm was now hitting him again. He was starting to understand why Lani had been so weird talking about her brother. There was something definitely off about Ben. Their parents had died in an accident a few years earlier, so Ben had always been a bear about Lani's safety.

Before Jakob could question his friend, Royal Jones entered the room. She was dressed in a Hawaiian print dress. However, from the look of it, it was what some non-Hawaiian designers thought a Hawaiian dress should look like. He blinked at the amount of makeup the woman was wearing. Most people probably wouldn't see it, but Jakob did. As an actor, he knew more than he ever wanted to admit about makeup. It was just odd seeing a woman who was already pretty slather on so much makeup in Hawai'i.

"My love," she said, her gaze moving from Ben to Jakob. "Please introduce us."

"Royal," Ben said, rising from his seat, "this is my best friend in the world, Jakob Wulf. Jake, this is the love of my life, Royal Jones."

Jakob called on all his acting abilities and didn't roll his eyes. The fact that both of them were acting so pretentious was a warning sign to him. Maybe it was because he had been surrounded by good relationships. Jensen and Nicola were so balanced, and you could never doubt their love for each other. He didn't know Alek as well as Nicola since she had worked for their family for years, but Jakob knew his brother-in-law was devoted to Jules. This seemed fake.

Jakob rose as Royal made her way over to him. She kissed him on the cheek, and he tried not to gag. The woman was wearing so much perfume it made his eyes water.

"It's so nice to meet you."

"Likewise," was all he could say before she started grilling him.

"Where's Lani? I thought she was bringing you here."

Her tone had turned cooler. "She had a call she had to take."

"What on earth could be more important than spending time with us. I have things about the wedding that we need to go over."

He said nothing for a moment or two. He had grown up rich, so he recognized this kind of behavior. His mother would have boxed his ears if he had done it. His gaze moved over to Ben, who was frowning now. Jakob waited for his friend to blast his fiancée for being such an ass.

"I'll find her for you," he said, kissing her cheek. Before he could leave, though, Lani stepped into the living room.

"Sorry, I had a call. What's up?"

"It was rude of you to waste time," Royal said.

She was talking to Lani as if she were a peasant. Again,

Jakob waited for his friend to correct his soon-to-be wife, but he just stood beside her, frowning at his sister.

"Sorry, but some of us have jobs with phone calls that require time. It was insane for me to do the job tied to Kingston Surfing in the middle of your wedding planning. But just so you know, it was a call with the caterer."

Jakob didn't miss the sarcasm, but apparently, Royal did. "Exactly. I was thinking that we need to change the flowers."

Lani blinked. "Won't happen."

"Excuse me?"

"It won't happen. It's too late."

He thought Lani would stick it to the woman. Jakob knew she had a temper. Royal opened her mouth to respond, but Lani forged ahead.

"If we were on the mainland, it might happen, but we are on Oahu, and they have limited supplies. Besides, it would mess up the bridesmaids' dresses. You don't want that because it would disrupt the wedding theme."

Damn, her tone, everything...perfect. He had forgotten that she was a lawyer. He knew they were using her in PR right now, but he'd heard she was also working on contracts with the aunt, who ran the legal department.

"Oh," Royal said as if that had not occurred to her. "You're right."

"I'm sorry. But you know, you could always have some kind of party when you returned from your honeymoon and use whatever idea you had there."

Royal's eyes widened, and a smile curved her lips. "That sounds fantastic. I will give you my ideas."

Lani said nothing, but he watched her closely enough to see her right eye twitch.

"Well, this has been fun, but I need to get to my place and clean off the grime of traveling."

The three of them looked at him with varying expressions. Royal looked irritated, but understanding lit Ben's eyes.

What surprised him was the relief he witnessed in Lani's eyes. She always liked to hang out with her brother, but he could understand that she wanted to get away from him right now. His behavior was odd, to say the least. He needed to grill her. Maybe it was just the upcoming wedding that had his friend acting like an empty-headed billionaire.

"I'll drop you off. I need to head out to a meeting with the organizers of the Kingston Invitational."

He nodded. "Sounds good."

"Dinner tonight?" Ben asked.

"I'd like that."

"We have reservations for seven tonight."

"Great. I'll meet you there."

They headed out of the house. He waited until they were in the SUV before he said anything.

"How long has your brother been acting like a dumbass?"

THREE

Lani's hands tightened on the steering wheel. "Dumbass?"

She didn't know what her brother and Jakob had discussed while she had been on the phone with Conner. In the past, Jakob had always backed up her brother no matter what. It wasn't like her brother did a lot of bad things to people or to her. It was just that she always got the idea that they were a team.

"Yeah," he said. "Taking off in the middle of the day. Scheduling his wedding with only a couple weeks before the invitational. That's not like him at all."

She sighed. "Almost since he started dating Royal." She stopped at a red light. "I'm assuming you're staying at the family home?"

He nodded. "And don't try to change the subject. I want to know why you are organizing their wedding."

Dammit. He was being a bear about that. She didn't want to discuss why she was being such a pushover. It embarrassed her. But there was one thing people didn't understand. They may have a big family of aunts, uncles, and cousins, but they had always been together. Before their parents' death, they had been close, but the tragedy had pushed them closer until now.

"Excuse me?"

Lani didn't look at him, but she felt his gaze roaming over her face. "Don't use that tone with me. I know you do that to avoid answering questions." Double dammit. "Royal was throwing orders at you like you were her assistant. Don't women get excited about getting married? Like the wedding part."

"That's misogynistic."

"Sorry. Women like Royal only care what people think of her. That is what I meant. And don't try to start a fight with me about that. You know I know the type."

"Yeah, I bet you do."

The moment she said it, she regretted letting it slip out.

"Now, what the hell does that mean?"

Well, she wasn't going to be able to push past this, so she might as well push forward. "Come on, Jake. You date those types all the time."

"Dating is sometimes a setup, you know that. I didn't know you paid that much attention to my dating life."

Someone behind them beeped, and she realized the light had turned green. Instead of questioning Jakob about his dating life, she started forward.

"I've been helping with the wedding."

He crossed his arms over his chest. "I didn't like her tone with you."

Yeah, neither did Lani, but her brother was in love. "She's stressed."

What she really wanted to say was that Royal was a major pain in her ass, but she only had a few more days left of this.

Then, she would get back to her regular work. She had a trip planned to Australia next month, and she was looking forward to it.

"What are you thinking about?"

She glanced over at Jakob to find him studying her. It always unnerved her when he would look at her so intently. "What?"

"You smiled, so I know it has nothing to do with your brother's wedding."

"I've got a work trip planned next month to Australia. It's been a couple years since I've been there. I'm taking a week off for some downtime."

"I do love Australia."

"Why does an Englishman want to spend so much time in the sun?"

She sensed his shrug even as she kept her eyes on the road. "I never liked the cold, foggy feel of England. We get sun. But it's different."

"Yes. I was there one April. It was fun for the first few days, then it got really boring."

He chuckled. The sound rumbled in his chest and sent little spikes of heat dancing through her blood. Why did the man have to be so damned sexy and somewhat charming?

"See. I love the sun here in Hawai'i. Australia is nice, but I can't get used to the upside-down seasons or the toilet bowl water. Also, there are a lot of things that can kill you there. We had someone bitten by a funnel-web spider on the set of *Wonderland*."

She nodded and said nothing. What she really wanted to say was that it had been his best work. The indie movie was released a couple years earlier. He'd been nominated for the role, and she had been so proud of him, but she said nothing. He had ensured she knew he didn't need her approval ten years ago.

"I take it that you'll be at dinner tonight."

Lani shrugged. "I guess so."

She felt his sharp study once more. He was always observant —more so than other men she knew—but this felt different. "What does that mean?"

"It was the first I'd heard of it, so I am assuming. I'll text Royal."

"What a stupid name."

She snorted before she could stop herself.

"You agree, don't pretend you don't," he said. "Was that her name at birth?"

"Apparently."

"And she's not originally from here?"

"Don't you follow her social media?"

"God, no. I avoid social media. All my stuff is put up by my handlers. I stepped back when all that rubbish was being bandied about Jules last year. I wanted to fight everyone."

That had been insane. She didn't know Jules that well, but her personal sex life had been splashed all over the place. The paps wouldn't leave her alone, thanks to her ex talking out of school about her. At least, that's one thing she didn't have to worry about.

"I don't blame you. I only met Jules once before that, and I wanted to kick her ex in the balls."

A surprised laugh exploded from him. "Same. Nicola convinced me to take a step back. I only put up quick pics or videos from sets to promote the movie."

"That's smart."

"Tell me more about Royal."

"Not much to tell. She's a couple years younger than me. Moved to Honolulu to become a pineapple influencer."

"What the hell is that?"

"Sorry. That's my term for all the haole who come here to promote living here without knowing the place. They make it look like you can live like you're on vacation. Don't get me wrong. There are some good influencers out there, even haoles, who talk about the issues on the island. But the girlies who decorate their houses to look like spas and pretend everyone can afford to live in Hawai'i are irritating."

He said nothing, and she realized that she had been ranting. "Sorry. I hate when people misrepresent Hawai'i."

They arrived at the entrance to his family's estate. It was much smaller than Ben's home, which had been the family home for as long as she could remember. Well, not anymore.

She pushed that thought aside.

"Code?" she asked.

He rattled off some numbers. After pressing them, the gate opened, and she drove in. She pulled into the circular drive and put the SUV in park.

"I agree."

"What?" Lani asked, turning toward him.

"I agree. I hate when people misrepresent anything, but I can guess it's worse here than a lot of other places."

"Why do you say that?"

He took a second, looking at her, his gaze roaming over her face. "Hawai'i isn't just a state. It's a culture, a people. Someone who disrespects the culture to make money isn't any better than the white landowners who stole the land."

It always surprised her when he said things like that. He was a man who came from a wealthy family. He was even distantly related to the royal family. But he and his family always showed respect in their dealings at their resorts. They tried their best to shine a light on the culture, and they tended to hire local people to manage their places. If they had been crappy to their workers, she would have heard about it. She did know that they paid some of the best wages in the industry.

"Exactly," she said, her voice barely above a whisper.

"I guess I should let you go to your meeting."

Guilt filled her as she looked down. "I don't have a meeting. I was just trying to get away."

His mouth twitched. "No blame from me. I don't think I will have much in common with Royal."

"Well, at least you don't live here. And you've been so busy that you haven't been here that much."

He looked out the windshield as if gathering his thoughts, then turned back to her. "There were reasons. I can't really talk about them right now."

She nodded.

"I'll see you tonight. Please don't leave me with them. Ben is freaking me out."

"I promise." Then she saw his expression. "You really don't want to be left alone with them?"

"No. And I don't want to be a third wheel."

"Gotcha. Okay, I'll see you tonight."

He looked like he wanted to say more, but he apparently decided at the last moment not to say it. She really wanted to know what had happened when she had been outside, but she would not ask. He slipped from the vehicle, and with one last look at her, he shut the door. She saw the woman who worked for the family come out to greet him, and he smiled at the older woman. Although she had lied about her meeting, she did have some contracts to work on, so she drove off. When she stopped by the gate and punched in the code, she looked up in her rearview mirror. Jakob was standing there watching her. Butterflies filled her belly, and she was thankful the gate was fast. She didn't need to be reacting to her nemesis/crush like this.

Pushing that thought behind her, she headed off to her apartment. She had a home office there, so she could work and think about Conner Dillon's offer.

"They may have to roll me down the aisle at Ben's wedding on Saturday."

Marta laughed. "No. You can eat so much food, just like your brother."

That was true. They had been blessed with an insane metabolism. His phone rang, signaling a call from his brother.

"Speak of the devil," he said with a smile. Marta stepped away to give him some privacy. He could have told her she could stay because the Wulfs never cared about sharing their lives with those who worked for them, but he let her go.

"How's Hawai'i?"

"Hello to you too, Jensen."

He heard a chuckle in the background and knew his sister-in-law was there. Jensen must have him on speaker.

"Hello, Jake," Nicola said.

It struck him then that not many people called him Jake, and all of them who did were close to him. Well, except Lani.

Nope, Jakob, don't be thinking about that woman.

"Why did you fall for my brother? He doesn't deserve you."

"I tell her that daily, but it is what it is," Jensen said. "Did you meet the fiancée?

"Yeah. Going to dinner with them tonight." He had gotten a text from Ben changing the time, claiming he had been wrong about the time of the reservation. Jakob told him he would text Lani the time to make sure that her brother knew she was coming. All he got was a thanks.

"What is she like?" Nicola asked, but something in her tone caught his attention.

"Why? Do you know her?"

"No, it's just...I know you're particular about social media. You don't always broadcast your location unless it is on set or an awards show."

"And?"

"You haven't seen anything yet?"

"Nicola, just tell him," Jensen said.

"Yes, Nic, tell me."

He had a terrible feeling about what she was about to say.

"Royal took pictures of you sitting with Ben and posted them."

"Oh. I thought it was worse."

"Well...the caption is what bothered me."

"What did it say?" He didn't even know her SM handle.

"Hold on, let me bring it up. Here it is. *Ladies, have you ever seen two more beautiful men? Lucky me, we're going on a dinner date tonight. I'll tell y'all about that later.*"

"That's weird phrasing, but don't worry."

"She's making it sound like you're in a polyamorous relationship."

It was irritating, but nothing he wasn't used to. Jakob was accustomed to people using him. Maybe he shouldn't be, especially from his best friend's soon-to-be wife. From an early age, he had learned that some people in the world would always see his family as a way to make money or get ahead.

"Don't worry. I'll let Amanda know about it, and she'll handle any worries." His assistant was excellent. She'd been in the business for over thirty years. "She hasn't contacted me, so it must be okay."

"I don't like it."

Nicola was territorial when it came to the Wulf Family. He was glad for it, but he also didn't want to cause her any worry. "I'll text Amanda and tell her to contact you if there are any issues."

"Okay."

And he knew then that Nic would text Amanda about it without being prompted.

"Nicola doesn't like her."

"I get that."

"No. She's been looking over Royal's social media as soon as she found that."

"I felt like I needed a shower," Nic said. "She acts like everyone can afford her lifestyle in Hawai'i, and she is disrespectful to the culture."

"Lani said the same thing."

There was a slight pause, and he wondered about it.

"How is Lani?"

"Fine."

"What was that?" Nic asked.

"Your voice was weird, bro," Jensen said, sounding like a douche. Then he chuckled. His brother had a weird sense of humor.

"Nothing, just, there seems to be something off between her and Ben."

"Oh. That's weird. I always thought they were rather close," Nic said.

"Yeah. And Ben was at home in the middle of the day."

"Well, he is getting married this weekend."

That would make sense if his sister wasn't doing most of the heavy lifting. He saw a glimpse of that when he was there, but Marta had filled him in on that situation. Oahu was like a small town in a lot of respects. Marta was on the Auntie network and was sure he knew more about what was happening with the Kingston family than the reporters in Hawai'i.

"Well, I'm going to jump in the pool for a bit."

"Okay. Check in with us, and Jules said something about jumping over early next week."

That brought a smile to his face. He adored their little sister and hadn't seen her in a few months. "I'll text her."

After hanging up, he headed up to his room. He always liked to be in the pool the first day he arrived in Hawaii. It seemed to help with his jet lag.

Nicola stared into space as she sunk into the fragrant bath. She had been there for ten minutes, pretending to read.

"What are you thinking about, love," Jensen asked her.

Nicola started because she hadn't realized that he was in the bathroom. "Nothing."

"Nope. I know you better than that." He settled down on

the edge of their massive garden tub in their bathroom. "What's bothering you about Jakob?"

She loved having a man who understood her well, but sometimes it was annoying. Knowing he would bug her until she answered, she set down the book she wasn't really reading.

"There's something about Lani. Always has been with Jakob."

He laughed. "Of course there is. He's in love with her."

Nicola frowned at him. "What?"

"The first time I met her—after I got clean, and we went to his premiere of *Getaway Car*—he gave me a hard look and said that she was off limits."

"Oh, that. It was because of her age."

He shook his head. "He kept reminding me any time our paths crossed. And she was nineteen when I met her."

"Still too young."

"Agreed. Still, I understand what he's going through."

"Oh, you do?"

"He's in love with a woman he thinks is too good for him."

Her heart melted. How did he still keep doing that after the past few years? "I'm not too good for you."

"Oh?"

She shook her head and bit her lip.

"How about I show you how bad I can be?" he asked, lifting her out of the water and into his arms.

FOUR

Jakob sat in the back of the family limo and waited. John and he had arrived ten minutes earlier, but Jakob still hadn't moved to get out of the car. He should have rented a car, and he would tomorrow. It was pretentious to have the family limo drive him around Oahu. Plus, he wanted a convertible. Jakob always felt everyone should ride in a convertible in Hawai'i at least once.

Thinking of convertibles, he thought about Lani's. The fact that Ben didn't seem upset by what happened with her car bothered Jakob. It was so out of character. And he felt there was more that Lani wasn't telling him. Her unhappiness was easy to see...but more, he could feel it. No one else noticed in the years since he'd met her, but Lani's moods often affected him.

He glanced around the parking lot once again. He did not see the SUV Lani had been driving earlier, so he waited. He didn't want to go into the restaurant and be alone with Ben and Royal. He hated that the thought even crossed his mind.

He and Ben had clicked as friends from the moment they'd

met. He'd been on the island to play a professional surfer, and Ben had been eager to help him portray the culture properly. That's why dating Royal was an odd choice. Hell, marrying her...he would have laughed in Ben's face just a couple of years ago.

Someone tapped on his window, and he started. Lani was standing beside his car.

"John, I'm gonna go in. Why not take the rest of the night off?"

"Are you sure?"

"Lani or Ben will give me a ride home."

"Of course. Have a good night, sir."

"You too, John."

She stepped back to let him open his car door.

"Daydreaming?"

"No. Thinking about when I first met your brother."

Her smile dimmed a little. "Oh."

"Yeah. When I came to the island, the one person in the world of surfing everyone said would be best to talk to was your brother. Kingston Surfing had a reputation of sponsoring some of the best surfers in the world and showcasing the Hawaiian culture."

She nodded. "We did."

"Not anymore?"

She shrugged. "He's changed."

The sadness he heard in her voice struck a chord in him. He did not like it one bit. He wanted to make her smile. Better yet, he would love to hear her laugh.

"Yeah, well, sometimes the right woman can still make a man do crazy things."

Like, sign a contract to act in a show based in Hawai'i.

Jakob was starting to realize that his motives might reach beyond career aspirations. Maybe the main reason was standing in front of him.

She glanced at the restaurant. "I guess we should go in."

"You don't sound enthusiastic."

"Yeah, well, my day started at five this morning, and I still have work to do when I get home." She pulled her attention away from the restaurant. "Video conference with folks in Australia."

He wanted to pull her into his arms and tell her he would take care of her. That feeling had always been there, even when all he thought he felt was lust for her. Jakob had wanted to shield her from all the bad in the world. Neither was ready for that, so he held out his arm instead.

"Shall we?"

Lani looked down at his arm, then up at him.

"I promise I don't bite unless a lady asks."

Pink stained her cheeks, but she took his arm. The moment her hand touched his arm, bare skin to bare skin, a spark seemed to flush through him. It had always been like this with her, which was one reason he had avoided her all these years. She smiled up at him, and his dick jerked.

Down, boy.

He might have some insane idea about winning her over, but pouncing on her in the parking lot was probably a bad idea.

They made their way into the restaurant. It was hard to get a table at this particular place. Locals and tourists loved it not only for the food but also the scenery. The restaurant overlooked expansive gardens. The lush greenery was on full display as people enjoyed their meals.

"We're here for the Kingston party," Lani said.

The young woman behind the hostess stand smiled at her. "Of course, Ms. Kingston."

Lani started as if she didn't think anyone would recognize her. She didn't realize how popular she was on the island. Ben had been popular when Jakob had first met him, but he knew that over the past few years, Lani had become the face of the company. She was the person most people went to. He might not live on the island yet, but Marta told him all the great gossip.

"Your party is this way."

He let go of Lani's arm as it would have been awkward to walk that way through the sea of tables. Knowing Ben, he got a table by the massive window overlooking the gardens. Still needing that contact, he kept his hand on the small of her back. As they followed the hostess to their table, he heard a few murmurs, but the truth was Lani could cause as much of a stir as he did. She was well-known on the island for working with charity organizations.

The hostess led them to the coveted corner and a massive round table. A niggle of dread settled in his gut. They didn't need such a big table if it was just the four of them. He wasn't the only one who was worried about the situation. Lani's spine straightened even more as she continued to walk across the room.

"Did you two come together?" Ben asked the moment they were close enough to hear him.

Lani shook her head. "Just showed up at the same time."

So, she wasn't going to rat him out. She left a seat open next to her brother. He pulled out a chair for her and waited. After a moment, she slipped into the chair, then he took the chair next to her brother.

"Kind of a big table, bra," Lani said.

"Well, Sienna and Rick are coming," Royal said, who had not said a word to them in welcome.

He felt rather than saw Lani's entire body go on alert. "Why?"

Royal's eyes narrowed as she studied Lani. "She's my maid of honor, and he's your boyfriend."

Before Lani could respond, she was interrupted by her *ex*-boyfriend. Which, he wondered, why didn't Ben know that they had broken up? Jakob studied the other man. It was Hawai'i, so people didn't get overly dressed, but Bellows looked like he'd just rolled out of bed before coming out. His brown hair was a tangled mess, and it looked like he hadn't washed it in days.

The other person with him looked vaguely familiar, like in a social media way. But then, a lot of the vapid ones looked alike to him. Her blonde highlights mirrored Royal's, as did her makeup and clothing. Women like them always reminded him of the Stepford Wives. Same hair, same makeup, same plastic surgery.

Sienna was frowning at Lani. Lani presented a serene air, but he knew better. Her hand was fisted in her lap. He didn't know what was happening, but one thing that irritated him was anyone upsetting Lani.

"Hey, Lani," Rick said, leaning down to kiss on the cheek.

Oh, that bastard was *not* getting his lips anywhere near his Lani. He blinked and realized that in a day, he had gone all territorial when it came to Lani. Partly because it was apparent to him that Lani did not want the surfer anywhere near her.

He stood and reached across to Rick. "Jakob Wulf. And you would be?"

Yeah, he knew how to cut people down to size. Not because of his time in Hollywood. He'd learned it at his mother's side. She had grown up poor, and she did not like pompous asses.

Anger flared in Bellows' dark brown gaze. It was quickly masked.

"Rick Bellows. I'm surprised you don't know who I am."

How had she dated this asshole? Maybe she'd lost a bet. Perhaps she'd had a drinking problem he didn't know about.

"I'm sorry. Is there a reason I should know who you are?"

The man's cheeks turned ruddy. Another direct hit.

"I'm the number one surfer in the world."

"Oh. Well, good for you." He tried his best to sound patronizing. His gaze moved over to the blonde at his side. "And you are?"

She blinked, apparently surprised that he didn't know who she was.

"Sienna Lawson."

Her tone told him that he should know who she was. He did not.

These people. Seriously. He had a passing acquaintance with the future King of England, and he wasn't as pretentious. And that was saying a lot.

"Nice to meet you." Then he sat back down. Yes, it was rude, but so was how she stared daggers at Lani.

Sienna looked at him, then at Royal.

"I thought you and Sienna would have a lot in common, Jake."

First off, where the hell did she get off calling him Jake? Also, the only thing he had in common with Sienna was blue eyes and the fact that they were both in the wedding.

"I wanted to catch up with Ben, plus, I wanted to touch base with Lani about the Pinnacle. Maybe doing a tie-in with Kingston Surfing."

Yep, he threw his sister and her husband into the mix. His family owned the resort. He assumed his sister would be okay with it since she was the one who told him to follow his heart.

Without having any recourse, Sienna took the seat next to Royal. That meant Rick was free to sit next to Lani. Jakob did not like that. It wasn't as if Lani was his date. Hell, most of the time, she acted like he annoyed the hell out of her. He had talked himself down from saying anything to Bellows until the idiot leaned over to whisper to Lani. Jakob wasn't someone who wanted to control Lani, but she stiffened. Oh, *fuck* that. It was all the indication he needed that she didn't honestly like the man near her.

Jakob leaned over, grabbed the edge of her chair, and shifted her closer to him. Lani's eyes widened as she looked at him like he'd lost his mind. "Sorry, but we have things to discuss, and I don't want people at other tables hearing them."

Lani was biting the inside of her lip to keep from laughing. And he wanted to be nibbling on that lip before slipping his tongue between them...

Her eyes widened again, and he realized he'd probably broadcasted his feelings. He banked his need before turning to face the table.

"It's been a while since I've been here. Any suggestions?"

Lani stared at herself in the mirror. She'd escaped to the ladies' room after dinner. She couldn't believe that Rick had the nerve to show up with Sienna, of all people. Rick had never been accused of having common sense. He was a hell of a surfer, but he always seemed to screw up his life.

She knew all this before they started dating. But she had been at a low point. It had been reported that Jakob was dating Gwen Hastings, his co-star in *Getaway Car*. They were at all the red carpet events together. It had been stupid to give in to Rick. He had been after her for months, and she knew he only went after her because of her position at the company. And they might have made it if he hadn't been fucking Sienna Lawson.

Drawing a deep breath, she exited the bathroom and found Rick waiting. What the hell had she done in her life to deserve this crap? She worked hard, loved her family, and did everything possible to make the world better.

"What are you doing here?" She didn't even try to hide her irritation.

"I wanted to talk to you."

"We don't always get what we want in life, Rick."

"I want to make this better."

This was not the first time he had said this to her. They had broken up six months ago, and at least three times a week, Rick tried to win her back. The fact that her brother hadn't noticed was embarrassing. Maybe he'd never really paid attention to her life.

"Rick, you're not getting it. There's one thing I can't ever forgive, and that's my boyfriend sleeping with someone else. I would also suggest when you do this to the next woman because we both know you will, maybe, not show up to a dinner with the skank you fucked."

"We showed up at the same time."

Yeah, like she was going to believe that. She'd lied about it to save Jakob from saying he'd sat out there avoiding her brother and Royal.

"If so, you should have been smart enough to know that showing up with her at the same time was not going to go over well with the woman you are trying to win back."

She brushed past him, but he grabbed her by the upper arm. His fingers dug into her skin.

"I will not give up."

"Maybe," Jakob's cultured voice said from behind her, "but you might want to take your fucking hand off her."

Dammit. She wanted to survive the night without being humiliated. Rick blinked and looked over her shoulder. "This isn't your business, dude."

Lani rolled her eyes. One of Rick's most annoying habits was lapsing into surfer lingo when he felt threatened. For some reason, he thought it would make him sound threatening.

"Is that a fact?" Jakob rumbled. She had never heard that deep, threatening tone of Jakob's except when he was acting. Looking at him, she realized he wasn't even making eye contact with Rick. Instead, his gaze was solely focused on Lani.

She twisted her arm, wincing because Rick still had a firm hold on her bare upper arm. He was holding onto her so tightly she was sure she would have bruises. Jakob's gaze moved from her face down to her arm. His face transformed from mildly irritated to rage. When he looked at Rick, the other man released her.

"I think from now on, you must stay away from Lani. She apparently wants nothing to do with you."

"I think that's up to her."

She couldn't help it. She rolled her eyes again. Turning her head, she made eye contact with Rick. How had she found him so attractive before? Yes, most women would look at him, see his soulful eyes, and think he was a good guy. But she should have looked deeper. She should have seen what a total bastard the guy was.

"I have told you before. I want *nothing* to do with you."

Then, without waiting for his answer, she stepped away. Before she could return to the dining area they were sitting in, Jakob took her by the hand and urged her into a little alcove.

"What?"

"Are you okay?"

She blinked. It had been so long since anyone had asked her that. At least sincerely. Jakob cared about what happened back there. Her brother, the rest of her relatives? They hadn't even realized that she and Rick were broken up.

"Yeah." She sighed, her cheeks burning at what she thought he might have overheard. "It's embarrassing."

"I can understand that, but who cares how Rick feels?"

She opened her mouth to respond when she realized what he had said. "Why would he be embarrassed?"

"Uh, you are definitely out of his league. That man should have been worshipping you. Instead, he did something stupid, although I'm not sure what, but enough to make you walk away."

Relief rushed through her. Lani knew it was stupid, but she cared what people knew about her life. She always tried to be a decent person. The fact that she'd picked such an asshole to date was mortifying.

"Your brother was making noises about ordering dessert. That's why I came to find you."

"Oh."

"But Marta made her famous pineapple cheesecake with that macadamia nut crust. I will happily share a piece with you in exchange for a ride home."

She didn't have to even think about that. "Deal."

He laughed and waved for her to step in front of him. They made their way back to the table. Rick was still missing and now Sienna was gone.

"I'm going to head out," Jakob said. "The day is catching up with me, and since we have a ton of things to deal with tomorrow for the wedding, I need to get my beauty rest."

Royal looked between them. "Don't worry. Lani can handle them."

"No, she can't," he said smoothly. "Plus, I have meetings to deal with tomorrow. So, I'll take a rain check. Perhaps in exchange for a dance with the bride at her reception."

Damn, he was smooth. Lani wanted to rage at Royal, but instead, Jakob had backed her into a corner.

"Of course."

"Lani's going to give me a ride home. I gave my driver the night off."

"Oh, I thought we could talk some stuff over, sis."

She frowned at her brother. "Work or wedding?"

"Work."

"I have a teleconference tonight with the Aussies, so I need to get ready for that."

"Why would you do that? I mean, you could have that meeting anytime," Royal said.

"No. The original time was tomorrow morning, but since you insisted on the final fitting to be so close to the wedding and insisted that I be there, I had to change it."

Royal opened her mouth to no doubt bitch at her again, but Jakob stepped in. "Must get going. Great to see you again, man."

Then, he hurried them out of the restaurant. As they stepped outside, a woman gasped. When she glanced over, she saw a teenager with her parents. From their sunburned faces, she assumed they were tourists. When the young woman spoke, her accent was pure Texas.

"Oh, wow! My friends will never believe I saw Jakob Wulf."

He slanted Lani a look before he smiled at the teenager. "We can't have that, can we? Do you have a phone? Want a selfie?"

The girl squealed in delight as she handed her phone to Jakob. Lani stepped back as the family crowded around to take a pic with Jakob. He glanced over at her and shook his head.

"Hey, folks, this is my very good friend Lani Kingston. Do you mind if she were in the selfie with us?"

"Kingston," the father said in the same tone of reverence his daughter had uttered Jakob's name. "Kingston Surfing?"

Lani nodded.

"You are looking at the granddaughter of *the* Benedict Kingston. I've known her for years."

The wife smiled. "He's a huge fan of your surfing invitationals. He can't surf to save his life, but he loves the stuff you do for the invitationals around the world. He's an environmental lawyer."

The man was still looking at her in awe. They all crowded around the camera, and Jakob snapped a few shots. Afterward, they walked to her car, and her horrible feeling from dinner floated away.

"So, we agree."

She glanced at him.

"About what?"

"I get a car ride home, and you get a slice of cheesecake."

She smiled. "Yes. Wait, no. I want one to eat and one to take back to my place."

His eyes sparkled. "You got it."

FIVE

As Jakob led Lani through the entryway of the Wulf home, which led to the open living area and kitchen, his nerves almost got the better of him. One of the things he used to do when on auditions was talking too much. It was one of his nervous tells. Right now, he wanted to babble his head off.

Why was he so bloody nervous? This wasn't the first time he'd romanced a woman. He didn't have trouble getting attention from women. Money and power were aphrodisiacs to many people. Add in the fame from his career, and he knew it attracted a lot of women. But Lani was different. She had known him for a decade and could see through his BS. He didn't even know what he planned by inviting her back to his house. He had just wanted to get her out of the situation that was causing her pain.

After they both slipped off their shoes, Lani followed him down the hallway.

"I've always loved this house."

He knew she had been there a couple of times. But it was one of the older homes along the beach, so they had not built it.

There was a good chance that Lani knew the previous owners. There wasn't a lot of beachfront property for new homes on Oahu. You either bought a well-established home or would have to buy one and tear it down to build another one.

"The view is peaceful. It's one of the reasons I paid a fortune for my condo. If I was going to be in Honolulu with all the traffic and tourists, I wanted a view of the water."

Her shoulders were no longer scrunched up, and she smiled softly. "That's better."

She glanced at him, then she looked back out the windows. "What is?"

"You no longer look stressed. You've been off since you picked me up at the airport today."

Her smile dimmed a little, and he didn't like that one bit.

"Maybe it's just you."

He snorted. "I would have agreed if you didn't seem so at peace right now. I mean, you *are* with me."

Another glance, this one from the corner of her eye as her mouth curved. Oh, damn, the woman was going to kill him with those looks. "You did promise me cheesecake."

He threw his head back and laughed. "That's something I like about you, Lani. You know just how to put me in my place. "Do you want some coffee with your cheesecake?"

"Normally, I would say no, but since I have to stay up for a meeting tonight, it might be a good idea."

He nodded and pulled out the French press and the electric kettle.

"Do you want me to help you?"

Her soft, lyrical voice jarred him for a second. He looked over to find her standing just to his right, less than two feet away. When had she gotten so close? Lani could be quiet. She was only about five-four in her bare feet. For a woman who could be so vibrant, she sure could sneak up on him. Damn, but the woman was pretty. She had always captured his attention, and every woman he had dated from the time he'd met Lani had failed to live up to his attraction to her. The truth was, he hadn't had a lot of genuine relationships. Most of them had been contractual. That was one thing the network had promised him. No expectations in his personal life. They would not get into his personal business if he didn't do anything illegal or morally corrupt.

"Jakob?" Her brow furrowed. "Are you okay?"

Great. He had been staring at her like an idiot. "If you could get the plates down, I'll grab the cheesecake."

She nodded and offered him another smile. Turning, she moved to grab the plates, and he tried not to notice the way her dress tightened across that word-class ass of hers. He failed miserably, mainly because his unruly dick kept getting in the way. It made sense since most of his blood had emptied out and headed straight to his groin. Thankfully, he had turned away from her before she could notice that he had been ogling her.

Once they got their coffees and plated up the cheesecake, they moved to the lanai.

"I miss being this close to the water."

He frowned. "What are you talking about?"

"I moved out of the house. I didn't feel comfortable with Royal there."

"I can imagine that. The woman leaves a lot to be desired."

She said nothing to that. Instead, she forked up some of the cheesecake. The moan that vibrated out of her throat sent his pulse racing. That one little sound sunk down deep inside of him, and well, a chap could only be so controlled. There was a good chance his cock would be imprinted with his zipper.

"That is the best cheesecake in the world," she said. She smiled at him, but it faded as he continued to stare at her. "What? Do I have something on my face?"

He shook his head as he continued to stare at her.

"What?"

"Do you happen to know how sexy you are?"

"Don't mess with me."

He cocked his head to the side and studied her.

"You don't."

"Listen, I get that I'm not the type of woman you go for."

Now, what the hell was she talking about? "Rubbish."

Her cheeks were pink, and she was looking everywhere but at him. "Listen, let's not talk about this."

"No, we *will* talk about it, because what you said is rubbish."

The sigh she released told him she wasn't happy. He didn't care. He opened his mouth to demand an answer. Before he could, though, she answered him.

"You date tall blondes with more attributes than I have. You have a type."

That was what the studio had wanted to see him with. Also, his former publicity manager. She had been adamant that he date what she said was the vision of American beauty.

"Can I let you in on a secret?"

"Sure," she said as she forked up another piece of cake. Thankfully, she didn't moan this time.

"Most of those women were contracted dates."

She frowned. "They were supermodels. And there was that one pop star."

Who had been lovely, but she hadn't really wanted to date him any more than he had wanted to date her.

"Yes. Supermodels who wanted to be seen."

"Are you trying to tell me those women only dated you because they were paid?"

He snorted. "No. I mean…look at me. I am a Wulf."

Her mouth twitched. "And you're so modest."

"Mutually beneficial."

"Oh, hmm, so you never slept with them?"

"Not all of them." And in the last six months, he'd had one brief encounter with a supermodel that had told him he couldn't ignore his feelings for Lani any longer. "You want to tell me why you and Rick broke up?"

"Please quit pretending you didn't hear my conversation with Rick."

He hadn't heard all of it, but he had heard enough to want to beat the shit out of the bloke. Though, Lani being free made his mission to win her heart easier.

"Fair enough. I didn't hear everything, but what I want to know is why your brother seems to not realize you broke up?"

She shrugged, but she didn't look at him. Instead, she stared at her plate as if it were the most interesting thing in the world. He reached out, slipped his finger beneath her chin, and gently urged her to look at him. It was always dangerous touching her, even with the tip of his finger, but he was done playing it safe with Lani. When he saw the tears, worry set in. Was she still in love with Rick?

"We broke up about six months ago, but my brother has not noticed."

He blinked. "A man who works for the company—is the

face of your company—was your boyfriend for what—a year?" He waited for her nod. "Seriously?"

"I kept attending functions without him, but Ben never seemed to notice. At first, I chalked it up to his wedding preparations, but when he had his engagement party, and Rick wasn't with me, Ben didn't seem to notice."

That was so not like his best friend. Again, he needed to figure out what was happening, but less than seventy-two hours before the wedding, it would be hard to corner his friend.

"I will admit that I took perverse pleasure that he hadn't noticed. I kept a daily tally for a while."

"Does Royal know?"

"I'm sure of it."

Yeah, there was a chance she did, and a woman who was as mean-spirited as Royal was, there was a good chance she did all of that on purpose.

"Are you still hung up on him?"

He waited for the answer, knowing there was a chance it could crush him. She didn't seem happy to see Rick at dinner.

She chuckled. "No. I'm sad I'm not as close as I once was with my brother, but maybe that's normal. Both your siblings are married now. Did that happen with them?"

He wanted to say yes just to ease her pain, but he couldn't lie to her. Not anymore.

"No. If anything, it's worse. My brother sends daily baby pics."

He pulled out his phone and showed her a pic of his niece, Maria. She smiled. Her whole face lit up when she stared down at the little diva who had Jakob twisted around her little chubby fingers.

"And I wish Jules would stop sending me daily rundowns of her pregnancy symptoms."

"No, you don't."

"You're right. Well, sort of. Jules went into detail about delivery, and, seriously, it was disgusting." He shivered. She laughed, and he felt as if he had won the Oscar, the Golden Globe, and a SAG all at once. That little chuckle meant more to him than anything at the moment. It left his heart lighter, knowing he had made her laugh. "I'll be seeing them probably on Sunday."

"I understand you ditched surfing tomorrow?"

They planned a day at the beach for the guys in the wedding party. "That's early in the morning. I have a tele meeting with my agent, and I need to catch up on some business for Wulf Industries." But he couldn't let his earlier worry go. "Are you sure you're over Rick?"

She sighed and rolled her eyes. "Yes. Sadly, I'm not sure how into the relationship I was in the first place. When I learned about Rick screwing all kinds of groupies, my ego hurt more than my heart. That should have told me something."

"Your ego?"

"Yes. There's one thing I can't take, and that's anything that makes me look stupid."

He could understand that. She'd graduated as valedictorian of her high school, and he knew she'd graduated at the top of her class for her undergraduate studies and law school.

"So, you saved me from dealing with Royal, Rick, and Sienna."

"That and I was ready to get out of there. The flight was starting to drag me down, and Royal and her friend were annoying." It had been apparent that Royal had decided to use her friend for two things. One to embarrass Lani. More than likely, she hoped that Lani would lose her cool and storm out. That's how he knew Royal didn't know Lani.

Her second plan was to get him interested in her vapid friend. They were both talking about the famous people they knew all through dinner. Jakob didn't get it, but maybe people not in the industry would be impressed. He wasn't just an actor. His childhood had been filled with playdates with royals. True royals. Being famous didn't make you more important than other people.

"You have no idea," she said. "But I feel like I owe you. I mean, I'm getting cheesecake out of the deal, too."

He blinked. Had he ever met a more beautiful woman? He didn't think so. He knew many movie stars and models, and yes, they were pretty. But Lani, her beauty came from within. It only enhanced her physical beauty more.

And in that instant, he knew exactly what he wanted.

"You don't have a plus one?"

She shook her head. "The truth is, I'll be so busy at the wedding I probably won't be able to sit down."

"Be my date."

Silence greeted his comment.

"I don't need pity."

The anger that vibrated in her voice set his alarm bells off. "No. We can help each other. You know Royal has some kind of idea that I want to meet one of her idiot friends. Rick wants you back, apparently."

She snorted. "No chance of that."

He cocked his head to the side. "So we can both act as buffers. You save me from the Insta girlies, and I save you from Slick Rick."

Her mouth twitched. "That does sound nice. I have too many things to worry about. I don't want to have to mess with his idiocy."

"So, we can pretend to be each other's plus one. Do you think you can handle it?"

She frowned at him. "What do you mean?"

"If you get seen with me a lot over the next couple of days, there might be gossip."

She rolled her eyes. "Sure. And they will just say you are hanging out with your best friend's little sister."

He should be awarded an Oscar since she didn't seem to understand the depth of his interest.

"To make it work, we have to sell the story."

She cocked her head and stared at him. "What are you after?"

"We need to seem to be interested in each other. Even just a little bit will keep Rick at bay. And let's face it, those friends of Royal are all intimidated by you."

Another snort. "Have you been drinking?"

"You really don't see how insanely amazing you are?"

Her breath caught. "Don't be nice to me."

Jakob laughed. "That's a first."

"I can't handle it, Jakob. I hate games, and if this is some kind of insane game you're playing with me, just stop it. I don't want to be friendly, then have you flip that switch again."

He blinked. "What the bloody hell are you talking about?"

"Never mind." She said as she quickly rose. "I have the early morning meeting and the stupid fitting, so I'll see you at the rehearsal dinner."

She was practically running away and leaving her extra piece of cheesecake behind. His first reaction was to stand there and stare at her like an idiot. Then, he hurried after her. He caught her right before she escaped through the front door.

"Hold up," he said, grabbing her hand before Lani could put on her shoes. "What the hell, Lani?"

She was looking anywhere but at him again, so he pulled her closer. He could feel her pulse thrumming in her wrist. Slipping a finger under her chin, he gently urged her to look up at him. Wariness filled her golden eyes. He had never seen another woman with her eyes. They pierced right through his soul.

"What's going on? You don't run from a fight."

Not that he wanted to fight her. Fight *for* her, yes. Although, he wasn't ready to reveal that.

"It's been a tough few months."

Pain and exhaustion filtered through her voice. He would have come sooner if he had known this was happening with her brother. Of course, when one is walking around with his head up his arse, it was hard to pay attention to what needed to be done. Lani needed support.

"I shouldn't have...just, let's forget all that."

Fragile. That's a word he never thought he would associate with Lani Kingston. Something was going on that she wasn't telling him about.

"This wedding... I'm happy for my brother, even though Royal isn't someone I would pick for him."

"Agreed."

"But if I say anything, it will put me at odds with my brother. Thankfully, I got him to agree to a prenup."

"He was going to marry her without one?"

She nodded. "But I got them both to sign. Still not as strong as I would have liked. It was better than nothing."

"How did you get that woman to agree to it?"

"I said she was protecting her assets, like her endorsements."

The Kingston Surfing empire was massive. "She believed you?"

She shrugged. "She's not smart."

He threw his head back and laughed again. "See, that's what is amazing about you. You get people to do things they normally wouldn't. And I bet you made her think it was her idea."

Then he sobered. "We can let people draw their own conclusions about us, but I'm not playing a game."

She stepped back from him. He wanted to advance and pounce, but he held onto his control—barely.

"Are you going to turn on me?"

"Turn on you?"

"You've been...rude to me for years."

It was the only way he could keep his hands off her. Neither of them was ready for that revelation.

"I was a dickhead."

"Uh...agreed."

He nodded. "And right there. I'm so sick of the bullshit that goes along with my job...with my family name. I know that you'll be honest with me. Ben used to be like that, too."

Her smile faded. "Yeah."

"Either way, it would be nice to be with the one other person who understands what a FUBAR this marriage will be."

She blinked rapidly, her eyes glistening. Jakob had never seen her cry, and he did not like it. His chest hurt at the site of her unshed tears. Then, before he could say anything, she straightened her shoulders.

"Okay. You got a deal."

"But just in case..."

Wariness clouded her eyes. "What?"

"Maybe a kiss...you know, just in case."

"In case of what?"

Good question. She was frowning at him, but he still wanted to jump her.

"Those girlies...they are tenacious. I heard Lucas Reynolds had one of them sneak into his house once. She was filming herself in his kitchen cooking like he had invited her there."

Her eyes widened. "I hadn't heard about that."

"He made sure it didn't make the news. Our agents work for the same agency."

And Lucas had signed to be in Jakob's new show. He had only met the guy once, but that story had come up.

"Oh. Well, I guess I'll see you tomorrow."

"Are you forgetting something?"

"Oh, yes," she said, her eyes lighting up. Then she slipped around him and headed back to the kitchen. He was playing second fiddle to cheesecake.

Before she could reach the counter, he took her hand and tugged her back.

"Why are you acting so weird around me? It's just a kiss. You need to be comfortable with my hands on you."

"There's no need. Remember? You said we would just let people make their own conclusions about us."

"No one will believe you're hanging with me if you shake when I touch you."

She was now. She shivered against him.

"I'm not scared of you."

"Funny, it sure feels like you are."

She looked up at him, her gaze locked on his. "It's embarrassing to say, but just know it isn't that I'm afraid of you."

"Disgusted by me, then," he said, leaning down and pressing his body closer to hers.

"No." Her voice was a whisper, and her gaze was on his mouth.

He should think of something witty to say, but he couldn't think of anything at all. His mind was blank. All he wanted was a taste.

She rose to her toes as he bent his head further, their lips meeting halfway.

Her mouth was soft and tasted of every temptation he had ever had. First kisses could be awkward, but this felt perfect. He wanted more...he wanted it all. But he knew he could only push so far. Scaring Lani off wasn't his plan.

Jakob pulled back from the kiss. Her eyes fluttered, then opened.

"I don't think we'll have a problem."

With considerable effort, he released her and took a giant step back.

"Yeah. Not a problem."

She took the cheesecake and walked down the hall. He saw her to her car, wanting nothing more than to pull her back into his house and take another taste.

"I'll see you tomorrow," he said.

"Yeah." She started the SUV and said nothing else before driving away. Jakob watched until the gate to his house slid closed behind her taillights. With his hands in his pockets, he wandered back into the house, thinking that a cold shower would be his best action.

He kept watch through binoculars. Lani was still in the house with Jakob Wulf. Anger slipped through him, burning his gut. She shouldn't be with that man.

His phone vibrated in his pocket. He wanted to ignore it but knew his partner would keep calling.

"What the hell was that mess?" his partner demanded. No, hey, how ya doing? Is everything okay with you? Just a demand.

"I don't know what you're talking about."

He did, though. Lani wasn't doing what any of them wanted her to do. That was the crux of it. Worse, she seemed to be slipping away.

"Want to tell me about the brakes on her car?"

Silence greeted his question, and he had his answer.

"I was worried."

"That she wouldn't die soon enough?"

That was the problem with his partner, who always rushed to grab the money.

"She doesn't have to die. She just needs to go away."

How his partner's voice trembled over the words told him what he needed to know now. Lani dying was the ultimate goal.

"Stop fucking up." then a dial tone.

He wondered when he got into the business of killing women but had a bad feeling that is precisely what he was doing.

SIX

L ani groaned when her phone buzzed on her bedside table at six in the morning. She'd hardly slept, thanks to the late-night meeting with the Australians. Worse, every time she fell asleep, she had that simple kiss in her mind.

She knew that Jakob meant nothing by it. The man did love scenes in front of cameras. It was nothing new for him. For Lani, that kiss sent sparks of electricity coursing through her body. Still, just thinking about it had her nipples hardening.

Lifting her hand, she touched her lips. She could still feel his mouth against hers. She couldn't remember the last time a kiss left her that dizzy or had her mooning over it. It was a little embarrassing.

Her phone buzzed again. That woman would just not give up. It was bad enough that Royal was forcing Lani to the dress fitting. And who in their right mind had a dress fitting the day before the wedding? A woman who changed her mind four times about what dress she wanted.

With a sigh, she picked it up. Royal's face was on the screen, and she couldn't handle it. Instead of answering, she set the phone face down on her chest and ignored it. There were only forty-eight hours of insanity left for her. Once the wedding was over, she would try her best to avoid Royal and her brother.

Her heart hurt at that thought. At one time, she and Ben had been close. Their age difference hadn't made a bit of difference. And when their parents died in a car accident, the two of them clung to each other. She had only been eighteen then and felt as if her whole world was coming apart. But Ben had stood stoically by, urging her to go to school. Jakob had agreed. He had lost his father a few years before their parents died, so she'd assumed he knew what he was talking about.

The phone buzzed again, and she rolled her eyes. Expecting to see Royal's face, she was surprised when she lifted her phone and saw Jakob's face.

Her nerves skittered, and her body heated. All her other worries faded into the background, and memories of their kiss came flooding back. Good God, this weekend might be the death of her.

She answered the call.

"Isn't it a little early for a movie star to be awake?"

He chuckled, a rich sound that she felt down to the soles of her feet. She curled her toes against the sheets.

"Remember, I just arrived yesterday. I'll be up before dawn for a couple weeks. Besides, if I'm filming, I'm in the chair for hair and makeup early in the morning."

She knew that, but her usual response was to antagonize him. "Did you need something?"

"Yes, but I have a feeling that's not on the menu at the moment."

She frowned at his flirtatious tone. It made her heart turn over and she got a weird feeling in her stomach.

"What are you going to be up to today?"

With a sigh, she grabbed the remote control for her shades. She settled against her pillows and watched as the view of Honolulu Harbor appeared. She missed the windward side of the island. She had lived in a little bungalow on the Kingston estate for the last few years. It was so close to the water that she could hear the waves when she slept.

"Lani?" he asked, his voice filled with worry.

"Sorry, didn't have a good night's sleep. I had that meeting and couldn't get to sleep."

"That doesn't sound good. You should have told Ben to handle his own damned wedding."

He sounded angry on her behalf. And yes, her brother should have, but she just couldn't let that woman handle the wedding. It was already ridiculously expensive and kind of tacky. Royal thought the richer you were, the more gold you needed in your wedding.

"Well, I have less than forty-eight hours, and then I'm free. I might even take a vacation."

It had been years since she had taken a vacation that wasn't at the tail end of a work trip. This time, she might just relax at the Kingston beach house in Kauai.

"You never answered me about what you're doing today."

"Oh, wedding stuff. Dress fittings this morning around eleven. I swear, there's no way I would have some big ass wedding. What is the purpose of it? It's not actually to show love. It's to impress other people."

Silence. He said nothing for so long that she was convinced the call was dropped.

"I have to agree with you. Both my siblings went the simple route. I liked that."

She knew that the Kingstons were considered royalty in Hawaii. The Hawaiian side of her family could trace their origins all the way back to Kamehameha. She wasn't sure just how much royal blood they had in the family line, but she knew there were members of their family who took it very seriously. They tended to want to make a big deal out of things like weddings. She and Ben had always avoided doing anything extravagant unless it was for the company. Well, until now.

Jakob was also royalty, but they seemed to align with her thinking. The public got to see so much of their lives. It was nice to have something private.

"Then, I have to head out to the resort. I have to check in with everyone from the caterers to the flower folks."

He chuckled. "Flower folks makes them sound like woodland faeries."

She smiled. Jakob always had a great chuckle.

"Well, I have to do all that, including making sure the rehearsal dinner is all set."

"Hmm, will you be on the phone to do that?"

"No, I'll go in and make sure everything is right."

"Where is that at?"

"Jakob Wulf! You don't know where the wedding is? How were you planning on getting there?"

"I figured Marta would know. Everyone knows about the wedding on the island. If not, Jules will know. I'm supposed to talk to her this morning."

She smiled. Yeah, that sounded like Jakob. For someone who came from what she thought might be a stuffy family, he definitely fit in with the Hawaiian way of living.

"It's at Turtle Bay."

"Figures."

She knew what he meant. It was where many wealthy people got married.

"Say hi to your sister for me."

"I will."

They both hesitated, neither of them seemingly wanting to hang up.

"Is there anything else you need?"

"I already told you that you weren't ready for that."

"Jakob, I told you not to play games with me."

He sighed. "One of these days, you'll realize that I'm not playing games."

She frowned and opened her mouth to say something, but he interrupted her thoughts.

"Oh, hey, my sister is on the line. I'll check in with you later, okay?"

"Sure."

"Have a good day, Lani."

Then he was gone. Lani lay in bed, staring out the window, thinking Jakob Wulf was still as confusing as ever.

Jakob stood at the kitchen counter waiting for his tea to steep, and he felt like a slug. He had panicked and lied to Lani. It was partially her fault, but he shouldn't blame her. He couldn't help but flirt with her a little bit. She sounded warm and cozy, with her lyrical voice all husky from sleep. He lost control of his mission. Lani didn't trust him, and he knew coming on strong was going to screw everything up.

So he lied and said his sister called. Knowing it wasn't the same, he called his sister to assuage his conscience. The moment the phone started to ring, he realized how early it was.

Didn't matter. Jules picked it up on the second ring.

"Good morning."

She sounded exhausted, and he instantly felt even worse. Jules was seven months pregnant with her first child.

"I'm sorry for calling so early."

"No worries. I'm just not sleeping well right now. Still, wake up at four in the morning, but this little one is sitting on my bladder."

He heard a deep voice in the background and knew his brother-in-law was nearby. He seemed to not want to be far from Jules, but Jakob understood, especially as they approached the due date. The truth was, Alek seemed to be handling it better than their brother, Jensen, had. He had been a bear about Nicola walking down the stairs...or basically anything.

"I'm fine. Stop worrying. I'll take a nap today."

Another growl in the background, and he had a feeling what Alek was worried about.

"Hey, why don't I fly to you on Sunday?"

There was a brief pause. "I miss you."

The sadness he heard in her voice was odd. From the moment they'd found each other, Jules had sounded happy.

"Is everything okay?"

She sniffed, and his worry escalated. Jules wasn't a crier.

"Yes."

"Jules, maybe you should wait until Sunday, and I'll fly over there."

"But I miss you."

The longing he heard in her voice hit him square in the chest. He thought Jules was happy in Hawai'i. She had sparkled anytime he had seen her with Alek. It was really disgusting, but he had been happy for her.

"It's just two days. I'll stay a few days. I think Alek would agree with me."

She sighed. "You're probably right. I just miss you. And Mother. And Nicola and Jensen."

He couldn't wait to tell his brother he ranked last on Jules' list.

Another growling comment from his brother-in-law, and she sighed.

"Alek wants to talk to you, and I must use the toilet. This baby hates my bladder."

"Love you, Jules."

"Love you, Jake."

Then, there was a jostling sound, and he heard his sister's voice.

"I can walk to the bathroom, Aleka."

It was another few seconds before his brother-in-law came on the phone. "Hey, Jake. Thanks for telling her not to come over."

"Is everything okay?"

"Yeah. We've just gotten to the point where she's uncomfortable in any position. Her feet are swelling, and she's been sad about not wearing heels."

He rolled his eyes. His sister had a thing for stilettos. "No problem. Nicola said she was surprised the doctor was allowing her to travel."

"That's another thing. I found out yesterday that Dr. Lee told her it wasn't a good idea, not even to Oahu."

"That seals the deal. I'll hop on the plane on Sunday."

Maybe he could convince Lani to come with him. They could spend a few days decompressing.

"Jake, are you still there?"

"Sorry. Still acclimating to the time difference."

"Yeah, it's a bastard."

"Is she truly okay? There's nothing wrong with the baby?"

"Naw, Jules just cries a lot now. Since about week twelve, I've had to be careful around her." He sighed. "It's been tough, and she seems to be getting worse. Her blood pressure is a little high, so they've ordered her to take it easier, but you know your sister."

"Yeah. I have some news I was going to wait to tell the family, but maybe I should tell Jules."

"Good news."

"She'll think so."

"Love, Jake wants to talk to you."

There was a muffled response.

"No, he has some news he wants to share."

Again, jostling of the phone, she was on the line. "I'm back. Can you get my tea, love?"

"Of course. Sit down," he heard his brother-in-law's order.

"Such a bossy bit of goods."

"But he's wrapped around your finger."

She laughed, and the tension in Jakob's gut loosened. "Yeah. He is. So, what is this news?"

"How would you feel if I moved over here full-time?"

"Here? As in. Hawai'i?"

"Yeah. I just inked a deal to be the lead in the *Task Force Honolulu* series."

There was a beat of silence. "That's brilliant."

"You're the first one I've told but don't say anything to Mother. I need to prepare her. She already misses you so much."

"You've lived in LA for the most part in the last few years."

"True. Except, I have specific reasons for doing this."

"And those would be?"

"Well, you're here, and I know that it puts me farther from Jensen, Nicola, and Maria, but they have Mother there. I wanted to be backup for you and Aleka."

"Oh, Jake," she said, sniffing. "That's sweet."

"I think I'll like playing one character for a while. Plus, it's in my contract that I get to direct an episode the first year, then two in the next...if we get renewed."

"Brilliant. I knew you wanted to direct."

"I didn't tell you that."

"Yeah, but remember when you did *Runaway Car*? You talked about Marty Reynolds and how much you respected his direction. You went into detail about how he worked. There had been something in your voice that told me you really wanted to direct."

Jules was the youngest sibling but was always the smartest and most observant.

"Are those the only reasons?"

"Well, no."

"I knew it! So, you *are* getting over your stupid rules."

"I have no idea what you're talking about."

"Come on, Jake, it's me. You've been half in love with Lani for years. It's the way you said her name. Wait, isn't she dating Rick Bellows?"

"No. They apparently broke up months ago."

"So, she's free to date. Good. You would make an adorable couple."

"Don't get your hopes up. I've been kind of an ass to her for years."

He could practically hear Jules roll her eyes at him over the phone. "Men. You were trying to keep her away because of that stupid rule about her being your best friend's little sister."

"It's out of respect."

"She is a grown woman. She doesn't need stupid boys making decisions for her."

There was a growl in the background.

"I'm fine. I'm just telling my brother he's an ass."

Another growling response and Jules laughed. The sound made Jakob happy.

"What's your plan?"

"Plan?"

"Yes, to woo her."

"I'm acting as her plus one at the wedding."

"That's it?" From her voice, Jakob could tell Jules didn't think much of his plan.

"She's so damned busy with the wedding. Royal treats her like a bloody servant."

"That woman. When you told me Ben was marrying her, I researched. Then Nicola got in it with me."

"Good God, that sounds dangerous."

"Maria had a fever, and they were stuck at home. I had just developed cankles—"

"What the bloody hell is that?"

She laughed. "My ankles are really swollen, so I had my favorite heels taken away from me, and I had to keep my feet up. We needed to entertain ourselves."

"What did you find?"

"Well, she's tried to latch herself to a few billionaires.

Mainly tech bros. And she seemed to be interested in a few athletes. One of those tech bros is Charlie Wellington."

"I thought he'd been married for years."

"Yeah. I think she broke up his marriage, but then he dumped her. It wasn't long afterward that she started dating Ben."

"Well, he's not a billionaire. The business is a family business, shared with all the relatives. He's beyond wealthy, but she might not understand. Lani said that she got the woman to sign a prenup by saying Royal needed to protect her brand name and assets."

"She's smart, your Lani. You know Alek's family features their brand in the surf shop here at the resort."

His brother-in-law's family owned a resort on Maui.

"She's not mine."

"Well, you must do more if you want her to be. Not just the fake relationship thing going on."

It wasn't fake on his part.

"Got any suggestions?"

"Well, since you are being mean and don't want to see me—"

"I did not say that."

She continued on as if he hadn't spoken. "What is she doing today?"

"Wedding stuff. I told you. Royal acts like Lani works for her."

"You should go help her. Or take her something like her favorite treat."

"That's Hawaiian ice. It would melt before I could get it to Turtle Bay."

"Hmm, is there anything else?"

"I'll figure it out. You get to rest, and I'll see you Sunday."

"Keep me updated on your progress."

"Sure."

Which meant that he wouldn't bother her. Not unless she wouldn't leave him alone through texts, which was a sure bet. After hanging up with her, he heard Marta arrive.

"You're up early," she said with a smile. She had worked for the family for several years and knew them well.

"I need some help."

"Of course."

"I want to take a friend—a lady friend—something. I plan on taking a piece of that cheesecake, but I feel like I should take her something more."

"Is she Hawaiian?"

He nodded. "And you can't take her to a place to eat?"

"She's busy at a location. I want to take her something besides Hawaiian ice, which is one of her favorite treats."

She offered him a smile. "Is she allergic to seafood?"

"No. She loves poke." Then it hit him. "That's brilliant. Thanks."

"Any time," she said as he rushed to get ready.

He knew one of Lani's favorite places to get poke was at a convenience store close to where she would be. If this worked, he would definitely owe his sister, but if it helped him with Lani, he didn't care.

SEVEN

Lani sat at one of the tables in the suite she had rented for the night at Turtle Bay. She wasn't planning on being there the night of the wedding. She assumed that she would be worn out pretending to be happy for her brother at the end of the day. It did mean she would have to come up to the North Shore again, but she would want her own bed on Saturday night.

The guest numbers were insane. They actually had over five hundred RSVPs. Thankfully, the wedding planner would handle the guests for the most part. But she was checking names against their security lists. They already had to inform one of the former Kingston surfers he couldn't attend. The guy was out on bail for domestic abuse against his girlfriend. It was why they had dropped him from their company. Lani still didn't know why he had been invited. Her phone buzzed, and she looked down at it.

Jakob: *Where are you?*

Lani: *I told you. Turtle Bay.*

Jakob: *No, where in the resort are you?*

She sent him the room number. Lani: *Rented it for tonight.*
Jakob: *On my way.*

Wait, what? Why was he on his way? What was happening? She was sitting there, holding her phone, her brain melting down because Jakob had contacted her once again. She had hoped that they would be surrounded by people when she met him face to face again. It would make it less awkward. Yes, she talked to him on the phone, but that was easier than seeing him and blushing.

Rolling her eyes, she set her phone down. Lani knew not to get excited. He was just being nice. The Wulfs were friendly people.

Five seconds later, she popped out of the chair to hurry to the bathroom. It was bad enough that he was surprising her. She was not going to look like an unkept mess. Her makeup was light, as usual, but she had been outside most of the day, and her hair looked like it. The trades were pretty bad today. Before she was ready, there was a knock at her door. She brushed her hair as fast as possible, then headed for the door. There was another knock just as she reached it.

Looking out her peephole, she saw Jakob. He was holding a bag and a box.

"I can hear you breathing."

With a sigh, she opened the door.

"I thought you might pretend you weren't here."

"Sorry. You just took me by surprise."

He smiled at her, and her heart skipped. It was probably a trite saying, but it was exactly how she felt. Her palms were sweaty, and her head was spinning.

Why was he so damn pretty? All of the Wulfs were beautiful. Flaxen hair, blue eyes...but Jakob was the best looking.

When he rolled out of bed, he screamed movie star with dimples and hair that probably looked perfect.

Oh, she should not have thought that. One, thinking about Jakob and a bed led to being overheated. Second, they were standing at the door to her room with a massive king bed.

"Are you going to let me in?"

Inwardly, she groaned. She'd been off since he had called her this morning. There was something different about him like he had an agenda, and she didn't know what it was. She had learned the hard way when it came to men to always know their plans. Still, this was Jakob, and he apparently had food.

She stepped back. He stopped in front of her. His gaze roamed over her for a long moment before connecting with hers again. It didn't make her feel gross like it did with a lot of men. This made her think...seen.

"You look beautiful today."

She snorted. "My hair looks like a tornado hit it."

"It looks sexy."

"Have you been drinking?"

He just chuckled. "The lanai? Since the trades have finally settled, I figured we could sit out there."

"Sure."

She shut the door and followed him through the room.

"These are nice rooms. Not as nice as those at Aleka's resort on Maui."

"I agree. I was there a few months ago."

He set the bag down and held up the box. "This is some cheesecake. You might want to put that in the fridge."

She nodded and took it from him. When she returned from her errand, she noticed a couple of containers of poke. She saw the label and realized it was the restaurant she had discussed at dinner the night before.

"You got me lunch."

"I hope you didn't eat."

The sweet expectation in his gaze made her stomach feel funny. She shook her head as a lump rose in her throat. This man was busy. Many people didn't realize how involved he was with the Wulf businesses. That, along with his acting career, he was always busy. He took time out of his day to do something just for her.

How sad was it that just bringing her poke was overwhelming her? It had been months since anyone had really done anything nice for her. Or was it just that she was overworked and stressed about everything: the company, the upcoming invitational, the wedding.

"Come, let's have lunch, and you can tell me what you've been doing."

He was once again holding out a chair for her. It was gentlemanly, and she was sure his mother taught him those manners. She didn't need a man to do that, but again, it was nice to have someone do something like that for her.

"Thanks," she murmured as she sank into her previous seat. He joined her on the other side of the table. "Can we talk about other things? I just want to get away from all the stuff. How's your family?"

He sighed. "Worried about Jules."

"Is something wrong?" She knew Jules was pretty far along in her pregnancy.

"No. Just, she's seven months pregnant, not sleeping well, and I found out from my brother-in-law that she's not supposed to fly right now. Not even the thirty-minute flight from Maui. Also, she was complaining about something called cankles and how she couldn't wear her favorite shoes. So, I convinced her I would go see her on Sunday night."

She chuckled. "I've heard a lot of pregnant women complain about the cankles."

"You're not eating."

"Sorry," she said, digging into her poke. "I can't believe you were paying attention to what I talked about last night at dinner."

"You would be surprised what I notice."

"Did you need some water?"

"I'll get it. You stay. You've been working."

Again, she blinked, but the sun wasn't hurting her eyes. She had to fight the tears that threatened to fall. It was a simple comment, but it was nice to be acknowledged. What was wrong with her? She was Lani Michelle Kingston. She didn't take any prisoners when she worked contracts. She could handle a press conference with ease. Almost crying because Jakob offered to get her water? Yeah, there might be something off with her hormones.

"Thank you," she said when he handed her the glass. He had poured a glass for himself as well.

"I do like how all the rooms face the ocean. I guess that's why they picked this as a venue."

"No. They picked it because it was one of the most expensive on the island. Or rather, Royal did."

He studied her for a second. "It must be hard not liking your future in-law."

"You definitely got lucky with both of yours."

"Well," he said, "I threatened to beat Aleka to a pulp when I first met him."

"The former Army Ranger who is trained to kill and resembles a Hawaiian god?"

He frowned. "I've been trained. And who gave him the title of a god?"

She laughed. "I bet he would have kicked your ass."

It only took a second for his smile to flash. With the beard he was sporting, it was hard to see those legendary dimples.

"Yeah, you're probably right. Mother forbade me."

She snorted.

"What?"

"Mama's boy."

"I am not. I just have a healthy respect for my mother."

And that softened her even more. He definitely loved his family. Even as she thought it, her phone buzzed on the table.

Aunt Rochelle: *I want to bring another guest.*

With a roll of her eyes, she picked up the phone. All the relatives were trying their best to get their friends in. This wedding was THE wedding of the year because of her family's standing.

Lani: *You can't unless we have someone cancel. It's a sit-down dinner. The final numbers were due a week ago.*

"What?"

She set her phone down and dug into her food again. "Auntie Rochelle. She wanted to bring someone else to the wedding. She's already bringing three people."

Before she could swallow her bite, her phone buzzed again. Irritation snaked down her spine. She loved her family, but they were getting on her last nerve. When she reached for the phone, Jakob snatched it away.

"What are you doing?"

"You are having lunch. Let them wait."

"It could be about the wedding."

"And it can wait thirty minutes."

Her fingers tingled as she thought about snatching the phone from Jakob. His laugh stopped her.

"What?"

"You. I can tell you're thinking about grabbing the phone. Take a few minutes just for you. You have one of your favorite meals, a gorgeous view, and a handsome companion."

"Oh, is Jensen coming? I didn't even know your brother was on the island."

His face flushed, and his eyes narrowed. "I didn't think you had daddy issues."

There was a beat of silence, and then she threw back her head and laughed.

By the time she could regain control, she had to wipe away tears.

"Tell me, Jakob, are you jealous of your brother?"

He sighed. "No. I just...I don't like your admiration of him."

She blinked. Was he really saying he was jealous?

"I'm sorry," he said.

"For what? Making me laugh. There's been very little to make me laugh these last few months. You did that, even if it was an asinine suggestion."

"Lots of women like Jensen."

"Yeah. But then, he's a Rough 'n Ready member, right?"

"How do you know that?"

The BDSM club was infamous on the island. Their membership was heavily guarded, but Lani knew too many people. And when Jensen Wulf showed up at the club, everyone talked.

"Everyone knows about the club."

"Are you a member?"

She shook her head. "I have friends, though, and I know May and Dee well. We do a lot of fundraising together."

The two women were the wives of the owners of the club.

His whole body seemed to relax. "Oh. Good."

"Why is that good?"

"I'm not into that scene. I went to a club with Jensen once but didn't like it. Although, I do like a little play, just not anything too specific."

Play? Like tying a woman up? Spanking? What?

That all rattled around in her head, but she didn't ask it. She couldn't. That would step over a line she wasn't sure she wanted to.

"Are you blushing?"

Yes. "No."

"You are. What embarrassed you?" When she said nothing but pretended to find her food very interesting, he went on. "I think it was the mention of play."

Her nipples tightened against her bra. Tension coiled, and she was sure her panties were wet. From just flirting. It was mortifying that this man could still do this to her.

"I'm not a virgin, but I'm not that experienced either. I'm also not used to you being so plain-spoken. So, stop saying things on purpose to embarrass me."

"I'm not trying to embarrass you. I'm being honest."

"Why? Why now?"

There was a long moment of silence. "I need to tell you something, but I don't want you getting pissed off about it."

She sighed, her heart sinking. Lani should have known that this wasn't really flirting. He wanted something. He wanted a plus one to come with him to the wedding. "What? Just tell me?"

"I was interested in you the first day we met."

"No, you weren't."

He nodded. "I was. You came out of the ocean like a Bond girl, and my brain stopped working."

"So you waited over a decade to tell me?" She rolled her eyes. "Am I *so pathetic that you must* lie about being interested in me?"

"What? No! You are not pathetic. You're funny and smart and sexy as fuck."

She felt her eyes widen because Jakob didn't cuss much. It sounded like he meant it, but he was an actor. Crossing her arms, she stared him down. "And what? You decided that after treating me like a boil on the butt of humanity, you decided to say that?"

"Dammit, okay, I've been an ass for years, but there was a method to my madness."

"And that would be?"

"I couldn't touch you. You were too young and definitely too smart for me."

"I...what?"

"You were underaged, Lani. I couldn't date you. My mother taught me better than that. And...I had an image I had to worry about, too."

His career had been just taking off, and she could imagine that dating her might have been a problem. Sure, other guys did it all the time, but Jakob, for being kind of a skank in many ways, wasn't *that* type.

"Well, you were mean to me. A lot."

He had done everything he could to ensure she didn't feel welcome around him. It had broken her heart.

"I had to. Whenever you were around, I was worried I would slip up. You tempted me too much. And I know that makes me an ass. It is completely unacceptable behavior."

"But you kept doing it."

"Because I'm an arse. It became habit, and the truth was, you are way too smart for me." He leaned forward and tangled his fingers with hers. Just like always, the spark of electric heat that lanced through her jolted her.

"You feel it, don't you?" he asked, his blue gaze watching her intently.

"Feel what?"

"That spark. Every time I touch you, I get seared."

She wrestled her fingers away from him and stood. He was saying too much, overwhelming her brain. He rose.

"I—I...you're freaking me out."

"I didn't want to do that. I just wanted to be honest with you."

"Why?"

He looked away from her, out to the ocean. "My family."

"Your family?"

He looked back at her. "You've seen how happy Jules and Jensen are, right? Hell, Jensen had been in love with Nic for years. I realized I needed to step up and be honest about my feelings."

"But you don't..." Her voice trailed off because she almost revealed that she had followed the gossip about him.

"I don't what?"

"Never mind."

"No, tell me. I can take it. I get it if you aren't interested in me."

"What?" The man had no idea about her infatuation. Really?

"When you were a teen, you followed us around, so I thought you had a crush on me. I get that you grew out of it."

It would be easy to confirm his suspicions. Just let him think that she wasn't interested in him. Yes, he was saying all the right things or at least admitting to an attraction. He was a living, breathing, broken heart waiting to happen. But Lani couldn't lie to anyone. Not to their face. And she didn't want to.

"I didn't grow out of it." He seemed to jolt at that and stepped forward. She held her hand up because she didn't want him to touch her. She was sure he would singe her flesh. "I need a little time to think."

He nodded. "I understand."

Jakob looked unhappy, but she knew he would give her that time.

"Are you going to kick me out of here?"

She shook her head. There was a small cowardly part of her that wanted to. She tried to pretend they never had this conversation. Her brain still wasn't computing his revelations. But she felt an insane need to be near him. In the last few months, nothing had been right in her world. That was until Jakob had shown up. And he had been the one thing she had been dreading. Another duty she didn't want to deal with. Now, he was a lifeline.

She shook her head. "I...listen, it's been tough with everything going on, and believe it or not, you make me feel sane."

His mouth curved, his dimples popping out, then his eyes

lit with happiness. "Then, I'll stay. Let's finish lunch, then I'll help you with stuff."

"Why would you do that?"

His smile vanished. "You have been involved with idiots. I also don't think you should shoulder the burden of this wedding. It isn't yours."

Something settled in her belly, a warm happiness that spread through her entire body. "Well, thank you."

He waited for her to sit down, then joined her. And there, with the light trade wind dancing over her skin, she sat in the Hawaiian afternoon and enjoyed lunch with Jakob.

EIGHT

J akob sat in the back of the family limo and readied himself for the wedding festivities and seeing Lani.

"Thanks for the drive, John," he said,

"No worries. Are you sure you don't want me to hang out to get you home?"

"No. I don't know when it will end, and I would hate for you to be stuck here all day. I'll get a ride home from one of my friends."

Truth was, he was lying a little bit. Jakob had one real friend at this wedding, the groom, who had morphed into someone he didn't recognize. The rest of the wedding party was Kingston cousins and the Stepford Instagirlies looking for a rich man. He wasn't being presumptuous. One of the bridesmaids said he was rich enough to afford her lifestyle. Brazenly...right out in the open last night.

Jakob stepped out of the car and drew in a huge breath. Sweet Hawaiian air drifted over him. He had loved the place since his first visit to Hawaii. Not just the beauty but also the culture. He had always been fascinated by how the Hawaiian people had protected their culture from every invader who sought to take over. You had to admire a people who kept to their traditions even as other countries tried to squash them.

He took his time as he made his way to the check-in desk. His entire body buzzed with anticipation. He'd spent the whole afternoon yesterday with Lani. They had spent very little time together at the rehearsal dinner, which had been boring and long. All the toasts had gotten on his nerves. Years ago, Ben would have mocked something like that, but now, he seemed to thrive on people kissing his ass. Jakob was starting to realize he might not know his friend. At least, not anymore.

He was on his way into the hotel to check in and get ready for the wedding. He couldn't wait to see Lani. Maybe it was because he had waited years for this, or perhaps it was because, for the first time in a long time, he was going after a woman with whom he wanted to build a relationship.

Before he reached the desk, his phone buzzed in his pocket. He pulled it out. His sister's face was on the screen, so he took it immediately.

"Is everything okay?"

She sighed. "Yes."

"But?"

"Nothing. I just... I'm bored. How do people sit in bed all day and not go mad?"

He smiled. They all had good work ethics that sometimes bordered on the unhealthy side. But out of the three siblings, Jules had the most energy. She was always moving, always thinking. He figured it was her creative mind. She couldn't seem to ever settle down.

"Read a book."

"I've read them all."

He snorted. "All the books in the world?"

She chuckled. "Sorry. I'm being a prat."

"You are, but you're pregnant and have every right to be."

There was a long moment of silence. "You sound better than you have in a while."

"I..." he sighed and stepped into an alcove. "I told her how I felt, and she didn't kick me in the bullocks."

"Honesty is always the best way."

And right then, he felt like a snake. He hadn't told Lani he had kept his hands off her all these years because of her brother. He would. One day. That is if she decided that they were meant to be together. There was no reason to drive a bigger wedge between her brother and her. His relationship with Royal had already driven a wedge between them. The last thing Jakob wanted to do was cause her more pain.

"I'm giving her space to think. I kind of freaked her out."

"You didn't pounce on her?"

"No! Why would you think I did that?"

"Jake, this is me. You've wanted this woman for years."

"How would you know about that?"

"It was the way you would say her name. There was always something there. And I saw a picture of you. It was you, Ben, and Lani. You were looking at her like she was your whole world."

"Huh."

He thought he had been better at hiding his interest. And he knew what picture Jules was talking about. It was a couple of years ago at the premiere of his spy thriller *False God*. They had been reminiscing about Jakob's first surfing lesson from the siblings all those years ago. He had wiped out almost every time. Lani belted out a laugh, and his whole world lit up.

"Amazing that no one else picked up on it."

"I know you well. I'm sure no one else saw it, but I assume I could since I've known you longer than all the jerks on the gossip sites. Plus, weren't you involved with Michelle Roberts then?"

He bit back a sigh. Even his family didn't realize how many of his "relationships" were fake. Michelle was a lesbian who needed to win more leading lady parts. He had fit the bill. What he never understood was why, in this day and age, someone as talented as she was had to do fake relationships. She had been nominated for an Oscar four times, two of those times before she'd turned eighteen. It was stupid, and she felt she needed to pretend.

"Yeah."

A gaggle of sunburned tourists wandered by. They were loud and obnoxious frat boys. "What are you doing?"

"I'm at Turtle Bay for the wedding."

"Argh, of course you are. Seriously, this baby is eating all my brain cells. It's annoying."

Nic had complained about the same thing.

"I'm about to hunt up the room they reserved for the groomsmen."

"Ah, okay. Have fun. Love you."

"Love you," he said. He hung up and turned and almost ran straight into Royal.

"I didn't know you were dating anyone."

How long had she been listening to his side of the conversation? She had snuck up on him easily enough for such a usually loud person. A sliver of unease slipped through him. There was always something a bit off about the woman.

"I was talking to my sister. Not that it's any business of yours."

Her eyes narrowed, and that vacant, stupid look dissolved into anger. Then, it slipped away. It was a second or two, but he could still feel it. The woman wasn't at all what she seemed to be.

Before she could respond, he heard someone call out her name. They both turned in the direction of the voice and found her friend Sienna walking toward them. Great. Just what he needed. Royal had kept throwing out hints about her friend being single the night before at the rehearsal dinner. He knew she was involved with, or had been involved with, Rick.

"Royal, there you are. I dropped you off, and you just disappeared on me."

"I saw Jakob hiding over here whispering into his phone."

He blinked as he looked at the calculated look in Royal's eyes. The woman was a piece of work. "I wasn't hiding or whispering. My sister was checking in because she was ordered to bed rest today."

"Is this the sister who is a nympho?"

The rumor Jules's ex-fiancé had started about her still pissed him off. And what woman used that term?

"Has anyone told you you don't live up to your name?" She blinked at his harsh tone. He was a nice guy, but he had a bad temper. He rarely lost it, and it usually was when people were being dicks. "No? Well, since I know a few of them myself, and in case you didn't know, the Wulf Family is in the line of succession in England."

Yes, about seventy people had to die, but that wasn't important. "So, I know what I'm talking about. You need to learn some manners."

He slipped away then, ignoring her gasp and her friend. Jakob still couldn't understand what his friend saw in the woman. She was mildly attractive, but she caked on makeup, which made her look garish compared to the locals.

He made his way into the hotel lobby. Having been raised in the hotel business, Jakob took in the resort once again. It wasn't a Wulf property, but it was beautiful. He smiled at an attendant who greeted him.

"I'm here for the Kingston wedding. I'm one of the groomsmen."

"Of course, Mr. Wulf," the man said, smiling at him. "Mr. Kingston has a suite upstairs. Here is your key, and the room number is written on it."

He tipped the man and headed to the elevators. He was still irritated with Royal and her nastiness towards Jules. There was something off about Royal. Who in their right mind would bring up those rumors about Jules, especially to his face?

The elevator doors opened, and only one person was on the lift. His heart tripped up a few ticks as he spied Lani.

"Hey, there. I was coming to see where you were," she said.

Jakob's brain froze. He seemed to have lost the ability to talk. Words. Those weren't coming to him. His entire body felt electrified by the vision before him. She was already dressed and ready for the wedding. Her hair was in a low bun, but two long tendrils had been left out, and they framed her gorgeous face. As usual, her makeup was subtle, but her eye shadow was darker, highlighting her golden eyes. Her lips were ruby red, and he wanted a taste.

But then...the dress. It was a simple dress with one shoulder exposed. The ivory material looked soft, and the explosion of pink and purple flowers definitely nodded to her love of her Hawaiian culture.

She. Was. Stunning.

"Jakob?"

There was worry in her voice. Good thing because he wasn't sure he would ever be able to talk again. She stepped closer, and her sweet scent seemed to wrap around him.

"Are you okay?"

That's when he heard the whispering. He turned and looked. Great, freaking people were looking at them. One or both of them had been recognized. Wanting...needing...privacy. He hit the elevator button again. It hadn't gone anywhere, so he crowded her back onto the lift, then hit the button before anyone could get on.

"You look amazing."

The furrow in her brow eased as a cute blush stole over her cheeks. Had no one ever told this woman how gorgeous she was?

"Thank you."

"I'm not that late, am I? I just saw Royal, and she wasn't ready."

She rolled her eyes. "She and her bridesmaids are running behind, but they are not my job. You are."

He blinked. "Excuse me?"

She smiled. "Sorry. I'm wrangling all the guys. That's why I'm ready."

"Am I the last to arrive?"

She nodded. "Most of the groomsmen stayed here last night."

And he had wanted to. He had wanted Lani to ask him to

stay, but she had not. Jakob had not pushed for it because he knew they needed time.

"I want to kiss you."

Her eyes widened.

"But I won't because I know it's about the wedding right now."

He leaned forward to whisper his next promise. "But once this is over, know I'm getting a kiss."

And hopefully, more. He drew in a deep breath of her heady scent, then he pulled back just in time for the doors to open. When they did, he found Ben standing on the other side, frowning. When he saw the two of them, Ben's frown deepened. Great. He wasn't in the mood to fight his best friend.

"What is going on?" Before Jakob could direct his friend's ire elsewhere, Ben turned toward Lani. "You're not giving Jake a hard time, are you? Can you just let it go one weekend?"

He wanted to box his friend's ears, but again, he would let it go. It's what Lani would want. Still, he wouldn't let her be chastised like that by anyone.

"Not at all. She wrangled me from downstairs and saved me from fans." Not a complete lie. "We've called a truce for the wedding. Her idea."

Ben looked between the two of them, suspicion darkening his eyes before his expression cleared, and he smiled.

"I knew I could count on you, sista."

She smiled at him, but it didn't reach her eyes. Ben was oblivious to it and her. Again, he wanted to grab his friend and shake him.

"Now that your best man is here, I have things I have to check on. I'll be back to make sure all of you are ready on time."

He didn't want to leave. He wanted to go help Lani. But he knew it would look weird. So, instead, he stepped off the lift.

"Save a dance for me, Lani."

This time, when her lips curved, her dimples popped out, her entire face transformed, and her magical eyes sparkled. "You got it."

Then he watched as the doors closed.

"That's good. I never thought the two of you would get along." He slapped Jakob on the back. "I think dating Rick has been good for her."

Jakob pushed away the initial surge of jealous rage that seemed to course through him. Just hearing the loser's name made him irrationally angry. He knew part of that anger was directed at Ben. How could he not know that his sister and Rick had broken up? He opened his mouth to respond, but Ben and Lani's cousin Hank called out.

"Come on, y'all. They want pics before the wedding, and you idiots aren't dressed yet."

"Let's go," Ben said. "I don't want to be late to my own wedding."

Lani's hormones were still vibrating when she stepped off the elevator. Jakob hadn't really touched her. All he had done was whisper in her ear, and she was a mess.

The moment she stepped into the common area, something pushed against her senses. It wasn't good. It was that feeling of being watched...intently. Unease slipped down her spine. Trying her best not to look like she was searching for anyone, she pulled out her phone and pretended to check for messages. All the while, she looked out of the corner of her eye.

Her phone buzzed, drawing her attention to it. She frowned at one from an unknown number.

Unknown: *You should be careful. Your life is in danger.*

What?

When Lani looked up this time, she didn't try to hide it. Her gaze searched her surroundings. She was now in the lobby area, and her gaze took in her surroundings. No one was paying attention to her, even though it was crowded. And why would someone want to kill her?

It had to be a wrong number. No one knew about her and Jakob, and they had barely kissed, so that made no sense at all. She sighed and pushed that thought aside because she had too much on her plate today. Hopefully, whoever it was found who they were looking for. The next message was from the catering director, who was freaked out. Lani shoved her phone back into her pocket and headed off to avert whatever crisis had arisen.

He watched from the other side of the lobby. Lani practically glided across the crowded space. It was easy to see the royal blood that flowed through her veins.

His phone buzzed, and he knew who it was. He didn't want to answer. Didn't want to deal with his partner. If he didn't answer, he knew what would happen.

He answered just before it would have gone to voicemail.

"What?"

"Did she react?" his partner rasped over the phone.

"Not really."

"What is it with this woman? Is she that obtuse?"

No. He had known her for several years and knew she wasn't stupid. It was just that Lani thought she could handle everything. And the truth was, for the most part, she could. When he first started observing her, he'd realized that the woman could juggle her legal work along with PR for the company.

"Not sure. I do know that sending it today is probably not a good idea. She has a lot on her mind with the wedding."

"Hmm," was the only sound over the phone. "I guess so. Still, I want to make sure that this is all wrapped up in a couple weeks. I don't want anything in my way."

He had always thought this plan was a bad idea. The Kingstons might be jerks in a lot of ways, but they weren't stupid. If anything, their legal position on certain things had been cleaned up by Lani. It would be hard to get away with anything against them. That was probably why his partner wanted to get rid of Lani.

"She needs another reminder of why she should run."

He would roll his eyes, but he knew from experience there was a good chance his partner had eyes on him.

"What do you have in mind? The brakes didn't seem to scare her."

He hadn't been too sure about that to begin with. Their parents had died in a wreck, so both of the Kingston children were fanatical about their car safety.

"Maybe another close call, but this time, it should be someone else driving."

"No."

"Yes, or do you not understand how much money you owe me?"

Fuck.

"Fine. But after this, you get to do the dirty stuff."

"She will recognize me. I can't."

"I'm just saying you do it, or someone else does it. I'm not going to do anything after this."

"Good."

The dial tone was his only answer. He sighed, knowing that this situation wouldn't end well for him.

NINE

About midway through the reception, Lani was done. Done with the relatives, done with Royal, and done with shoes.

She leaned against the wall, watching other people dance. Most everyone was having a good time, and she felt like an ass for being grumpy. She blamed it on her stupid shoes. Glaring down at her feet, she wondered what would happen if she yanked them off and ran away. Not that she was thinking about actually doing that. Not really.

She had picked a location that kept her out of sight of the head table. Heels usually didn't bother her, but she didn't wear these insane three-inch stilettos. She should have gone with the flats she had eyed. Instead, Lani did it to appease Royal because the bride wanted everyone to wear heels. Lani didn't consider herself part of the wedding party, but Royal did. Not enough for her to sit at the head table or be part of the wedding.

Her stomach grumbled. Yep, she hadn't eaten since breakfast. There was a good chance she would gnaw off the face of the next person who stepped up to bother her.

"Why aren't you sitting at the big table up front?" Jakob asked, his breath feathering over her sensitive ear.

Oh, well, now, she wasn't about to do anything to his pretty face.

She glanced over at him. How did he sneak up on her? And just where was his partner for the night?

"The maid of honor got my seat."

Or that is what Royal claimed.

"What the hell?"

She shrugged and tried to ignore the way he looked. The man was made to wear a tux. It looked like it had been custom-made for him, which made sense since he had bought one just for this occasion.

"Lani?"

She blinked, realizing she was staring up at him like an idiot. Yep, she was sure that she looked like an idiot.

"What did you ask? Sorry? Blood sugar is low."

Her aunt had brought the extra person, as did a few other family members. Any no-shows and extra meals were snapped up.

His frown darkened, and even in his irritation, he was gorgeous. His face flushed, and his eyes narrowed.

"Did you not eat?"

She shook her head and opened her mouth to explain, but he didn't give her time.

"What do you want?"

She blinked. "What?"

"What do you want? Steak, salmon, whatever, tell me."

"You don't have to do that, Jake."

His eyes darkened. They seemed to do that any time she called him by the nickname. "No, *I* don't. Your dumbass brother should be wondering why you hadn't eaten. Either way, I want to make sure you're fed." The cake had been cut, and the toasts had been given, so neither had a reason to be there anymore. "Which restaurant do you like here?"

She shrugged. "All of them are decent."

"I'm going to beg off. Tell your brother that I have to call my sister or something. Meet me in the lobby, and we'll decide."

She should stay. She shouldn't run off with Jakob, but she had done her part. From the moment her brother started dating Royal, she had been the dutiful sister. When he had sprung the wedding on her, then dumped everything into her lap, she had done what she needed to do. It had always been the two of them, and she felt he might realize his mistake. Or maybe his love would change Royal. Instead, it had changed him.

"Lani?"

She blinked again and nodded. "I'll meet you there."

Then, he kissed her cheek and strode away. She lifted her hand and brushed her fingers over her cheek. He'd kissed her as if it was the most normal thing to do. Her head spun with the turnabout the last few days had brought her. Lani wasn't a woman who leaped into a relationship or even a situationship without thinking about it for a long time.

No, that was wrong. There had been one guy, and her ego was still reeling from that fallout.

As if to remind her the universe put Rick in her path.

"Hey, Lani. I thought we could talk."

The man had lost his mind. He didn't get it. Still, she understood her dumping him had been a blow. Rick wasn't a man who got left by women. That was all this was, and she didn't want to deal with it. Lani also didn't want to have a scene at her brother's wedding. It would make it harder to disappear.

"I don't have time right now. I have to check on something for Royal."

The lie rolled right off her tongue as if it were second nature. Yes, there were times she had to be careful about what she said in public. She was the head of PR, so she understood there were gray areas in business. But in her personal life, she rarely lied and never thought she would be that good at it.

At first, she thought Rick knew she was lying. His eyes narrowed, then his expression relaxed into what he thought was a charming smile. She had felt the same thing at one time. Now, though, he looked like a shark ready to attack.

"After?"

She wanted to tell him to fuck off. She wasn't someone who used a lot of profanity. It came from going to a Catholic elementary school and having an aunt who was a nun. So, the thought almost made her laugh. Instead, she gave him a smile. "I'll find you."

He smiled. There was that same dimpled grin that had first captured her attention. None of the surfers had ever really paid attention to her past the business they had together. She usually would say she wasn't the type they went for. But Rick had been different. He had asked her out the first day they'd met.

Rick leaned closer as if to kiss her on the cheek, but she pretended not to notice and moved away. "Give me about thirty minutes," she said as she hurried away. Her cheeks were burning from her deception. That was why she was never a good liar. She blushed.

Thankfully, she hurried out of the reception without a backward glance. She didn't want to see if Rick was watching her, and she didn't want to make eye contact with her brother. She was sure he would question where she was going if she did.

Her stomach muscles clenched, but someone grabbed her arm when she thought she was cleared of everyone. She looked behind her, ready to smack the person who dared to touch her without permission, and found herself face-to-face with Jakob.

"What did surfer boy want?"

"He wanted to talk. I said I would be back in thirty minutes."

"Not bloody likely."

She snorted. "I know. I'm not coming back tonight."

"You're not staying here?"

She shook her head.

"That opens the possibilities of places to eat. Let's go."

She had her purse with her. "We can take that behemoth of a vehicle. Let's go."

Thankfully, they avoided anyone from her family or interested parties. However, she couldn't be sure some tourist hadn't seen Jakob and snapped a pic. Currently, she didn't care. All she knew was that he was rescuing her from hunger and having to deal with her idiot ex.

They were waiting at the valet stand when she felt his attention her. She looked over at him. "What?"

"I just never get used to your beauty. It stuns me that you seem to grow more beautiful every time I see you."

She blinked at him, then shook her head. "You don't have to compliment me, Jakob."

His eyes narrowed. "As I have said before, you have dated stupid men."

"True story." She saw the valet returning with the SUV. "How about you drive? My feet are hurting, and I just want to collapse."

He nodded. "Anything you ask."

She was opening her purse to tip the valet, but Jakob had already tipped the guy before she could pull out any cash. Once they were in the car, she slipped off her shoes. "So, what do you want? I guess we could have stayed at the hotel to eat."

She shook her head as he drove down the long driveway that led out of the resort. "Naw, you know what I want. Some local cuisine, like Zippy's or Rainbow. Or Sidestreet Inn."

"Tell me which one, and I will take you there."

She smiled. "Great, you're gonna want to get on Kam Highway."

Thirty minutes later, they were sitting in a Zippy's eating. Jakob had been there once or twice in his travels, but it was definitely interesting to be there with Lani. She'd insisted on the Mililani location because she said it was her favorite. There was a smattering of people in the place, but no one seemed to pay attention to them.

She was smiling at him, holding up a SPAM musubi. He liked the smiling, which was much better than the frowns she usually threw his way.

"Jake, come on. Try it."

SPAM, ugh. He was not about to eat that. The idea disgusted him.

"One bite, and I'll let it go."

Her eyes were sparkling, and her whole face lit up with...he didn't know what. It was just good to see that she wasn't so stressed anymore. He sighed and took it from her.

"One bite."

Then he took a bite. The hit of seaweed with the sweet rice, then the salty SPAM, was surprisingly delicious.

She laughed. "You like it. Before long, you'll finally try moco loco."

He made a face. "No. I can't handle eggs sunny side up. Or just...no. It has to be well cooked."

Jakob took another little nibble as she scooped up her saimin. The Hawaiian noodle soup smelled delicious, but he was not hungry. He had gotten dinner.

"What are your plans tomorrow?"

She shrugged. "I'm having some kind of lunch with my brother and Royal."

"You don't know what it is?"

"No. I know what it is. I'm surprised he didn't invite you so you could spend time with Sienna."

It was even more evident at the wedding that Royal wanted him to be interested in the woman. She was nice enough and definitely pretty in that Instagram model way. But...she just couldn't compare to Lani. And it made no sense because Sienna seemed to be enamored with Rick.

"I've been hearing rumors."

He cocked his head. "You should never listen to rumors."

"There's a new show that's being set in Hawaii."

He shouldn't be surprised. Ben was the face of Kingston Surfing. Everyone who paid attention knew that Lani was the brains behind a lot of it. She also had all the connections.

"Is there?"

Irritation moved over her expression, and he almost laughed. It was so much fun to mess with her. "Jakob. Tell me."

He sighed. "I'm not supposed to say anything."

"Which is an answer. Is it finalized?"

He nodded. "The rest of the cast isn't set yet."

She ate a little more of her saimin. "So you're going to move over here. Going to live in your family's house?"

He shook his head. "I thought about it, but I would be in the way whenever someone comes over. Also, when I'm filming, I can have insane hours. Most of the filming will probably be in and around Honolulu."

"That makes sense. It's not that far, but you could get stuck if there is an accident or weather issue."

"Where are you living?"

"I bought a condo by Ward Center. It's a little busy, but it has a killer view."

Then she started eating again, and he enjoyed watching her. When she realized he was watching her, she made a face. "What?"

He shook his head, unable to put into words exactly what he felt. It was nice to hang out with nobody bothering them, and no older brother giving him accusing looks. Not that Ben would notice his attention these days.

"Do you think they'll last?"

She shrugged. "Probably as long as Ben doesn't realize."

"Realize what?"

"That she's probably cheating on him. Not that I know anything, but when I walk into a room, and she whispers into the phone and hangs up, it makes me suspicious."

"Did you say anything to Ben?"

"No. I have no proof, and I tried to get him to wait a year or at least six more months before the wedding. He wouldn't."

His friend had really gone off the deep end. Not that Jakob didn't believe in happily ever after. His siblings had met and married their soulmates, so he understood. But he agreed with Lani. There was something off.

He didn't want to think about that anymore. He didn't want to worry that his friend just screwed up his life, either.

"So, what do you want to do?"

"Truthfully?"

He nodded.

"I want to get out of this, get up, put on my comfy clothes, and watch something fun."

"Want company? Or...we could go to my place. I'm sure we could find something for you and do a marathon of something. I'll even watch *Gilmore Girls*."

"Why would I watch that?"

"It is always Jules's go-to for comfort."

"Oh. Well, not my thing." She searched his gaze for a moment, and a smile spread across her face. Her lips curled, her eyes brightened, and Jakob felt he owned the world. "I saw that you really liked *Only Murders in the Building*."

For a moment, he was surprised. "Have you been reading my interviews?"

Heat filled her cheeks, and apparently, he loved when she blushed. "Maybe."

"I have not watched the newest season."

"I haven't either. I've been too busy with the wedding and the invitational."

He was trying not to get too excited. "Since you aren't staying at the resort, do you want to go back to your place and change?"

She shook her head. The smile she sent him had his dick pressing against his zipper. Thank God they were sitting down, so he didn't embarrass himself. She had rarely smiled at him over the years, but when she did, he felt like he was standing in the sunshine. It was oddly comforting and unsettling at the same moment. The panic he felt was all his own doing. He worried he would do something to get her to stop looking at him with that smile.

"I have clothes in the SUV since I stayed at the resort last night. I noticed that you didn't book a room at the resort."

He shrugged, not sure just how to explain it.

"It can look odd sometimes if I stay at a resort. Plus..." he let his voice trail off, not wanting to offend her.

"Plus, what?" Lani asked before using her chopsticks to scoop up some more noodles.

"I wanted to avoid people."

She chewed her noodles and swallowed, her golden gaze locked onto his face.

"I didn't realize we had so much in common. I mean, I love people. I get that parties are fun, and I like to get together with friends and family. It's just that sometimes, I need a break."

He nodded, feeling a little lighter. It was nice to be understood. "When everyone watches you, making one move can cause many issues. Jensen had issues with it to some extent. Especially during his years as a user."

During those dark days, Jensen always caused problems for the family. Thankfully, he'd gotten sober, and their mother had hired Nic to be his sober companion. The rest was history.

"And everything your sister went through. That bastard Gregor should be in prison for what he did to her."

"No, him being ostracized by everyone is better. He's in prison of his own making."

"True."

She looked out the window at that moment, and he felt her pulling away.

"Lani?"

It took her a second or two before she finally turned to look at him.

"You're a good brother."

And even though she didn't say it, she meant hers wasn't.

"He'll get his head out of his arse soon."

"Hopefully. Even so, I've looked into other opportunities."

Alarm lit through him. "You're not leaving Hawaii."

She shook her head. "No. Those years I spent on the mainland taught me that while I loved exploring different places, Hawaii would always be my home."

"So, what are you talking about?"

She bit her lower lip. The woman was trying to kill him.

"You promise not to say anything to Ben?"

He nodded.

"There have been a few companies that have tried to hire me away. Most of the time, I ignore them because they would require me to move. One just came up, though that's based here in Hawaii."

"Another surfing company?"

"Oh, no. There is no way I would do that. This would be for a security company. They want someone to head up their legal department here. They're based in Miami, but the company is growing fast, and they need someone on-site to handle their legal matters in the Pacific Rim."

"And you have that background."

Of course, someone saw her and wanted to poach her. Lani was brilliant.

"I don't do legal work for Kingston."

"Lani, this is me. I know that you handle more than PR. I also know that you graduated with honors." Then he started thinking about what she had said about the company in question. "Are you talking about Dillon Security?"

Her eyes widened. "How did you guess?"

"They handle our security. We had them thoroughly checked out."

"Well, I haven't even met with Conner."

"But you will?"

She nodded. "Tuesday. We're just having lunch. I never thought I would leave the company, but I'm not sure what will happen with Royal at my brother's side. And there is no way I am going to stay in PR."

"Wait, I thought you would move into legal soon."

"That was the plan, but Royal is still making noises about moving the company to the mainland."

He frowned. "The family would never go for it."

"No, they wouldn't. There will be a board vote."

And the pain he witnessed in her gaze told him everything. She would be forced to choose between the business and her brother.

"If you leave, you will still be on the board."

She nodded. "But it will be easier."

To side with her family over her brother. She left that unsaid, but he knew what she was implying.

"Also, Conner just wants to meet for lunch and talk. Nothing may come of it."

He wanted to ask more but knew it wasn't the right time.

"Are you done?"

She nodded, and they took their trays to the trash bin. Then, he led her to the door, holding it open for her. Just like when they walked into the restaurant a few nights before, he settled his hand on the small of her back. It was one of those things he needed to do on some primal level.

He took her to the SUV, and she paused to look over her shoulder.

"What?"

"Do you feel like someone is watching us?" she asked, her gaze moving over the parking lot. It wasn't particularly busy that time of night.

"No, but I'm accustomed to people watching me."

Understanding lit her eyes. "Yeah, I can understand that."

He helped her in, then hurried around the hood of the car and climbed in.

"Ready for some murder and mayhem with the oddest trio that ever worked in a show before?"

She laughed. "Yes. I need to escape, even for a little while."

And with that, he pulled out of the parking lot. He would not screw tonight up.

TEN

A bout an hour later, they arrived at his family's home.
Anticipation left Lani feeling out of sorts but strangely
calm. She should be on edge, but for some reason, this felt
completely normal to her. He unlocked the front door and
stepped inside first to turn off the alarm.

"Did you want to change?" he asked.

"Do you mind if I jump in the shower?"

He blinked. It was a slow movement, almost as if it was
some kind of movie slow-motion sequence. Or maybe it was
her. Maybe she had lost her damned mind, and she was actually
imagining it. Either way, those long lashes, and his mesmerizing
eyes held her captive for the moment. In the next instant, his
cheeks flushed. The look was so cute. Was he actually blushing
because she asked to take a shower?

"Of course. The bathroom downstairs doesn't have a
shower. You can use the master's upstairs."

"I don't want to take your bathroom."

"No worries. I can get changed in another room."

He motioned with his head toward the open staircase that

led to the upstairs. She followed him up the stairs, trying her best not to concentrate on his ass. Seriously, did the man work out every freaking day? Even in dress pants, it was impressive. Definitely could bounce a quarter off of it.

She blinked. When did she start thinking things like that? Well, since that kiss...but if she were truthful with herself, she had always thought that way about Jakob. From the moment she'd met him, her hormones seemed to be in tune with him. Lani always had to fight the urge to jump his bones. For years, it had been easy because he always acted like he didn't want her around. Now? Yeah, now that was a problem because he was being nice to her, kissed her twice, and they were alone in his house.

She had never seen the master bedroom, but the moment she stepped into it, her entire body sighed. It was large and airy, with a massive king-size bed. Jakob walked over to the French doors. After unlocking them, he pulled them open, and her breath caught.

Lani had been born and raised on Oahu, but she would be forever in awe of the beauty. It was dark out, but she could hear the surf down below. She set her bag on the bed and walked to the balcony. When Jakob moved away from her, she wondered about it but pushed the thought aside for now. Instead, she kept her attention on the landscape.

The balcony overlooked the lit pool. It wasn't a massive house with much land, but the view. Nothing could compare, not for her. She had been all over the world, but nothing spoke to her like the sound of the surf, the smell of the ocean, and the feeling of belonging. Only Hawaii did that for her.

"I'm going to grab something to wear and get out of your hair."

She turned to give him her attention. He was at the dresser, rifling through one of the drawers.

"What's wrong?"

"Nothing."

He bit off the word, and she frowned.

"Jake. It's me. Don't revert to your old self. Tell me what's going on."

He released a sigh that was filled with trepidation. "We're in here, and you're acting like it's normal."

He still hadn't looked at her, not even in the mirror.

Worry set in her belly. Was he regretting this? Did he want her to leave?

"What's not normal?"

His shoulders seemed to drop, and he turned to face her again. Even in the darkened room, the moon gave her enough light to see his expression.

"You. That bed. Everything."

She was even more confused and opened her mouth to say just that. Instead, Jakob took two big steps toward her and grabbed her by the arms. Yanking her forward, he bent his head and slammed his mouth down on hers. For a moment, she didn't react. How could she? Jakob Wulf, the man of all her fantasies, was kissing her like his life depended on it.

Then, heat blasted through her in one split second, rushing along her veins like an inferno. She slipped her hands up his chest and over his shoulders as she answered his kiss with everything she had. He pressed her closer, letting her feel the long, thick length of him. Her entire body lit up, her blood heating, her nipples hardening, and her sex flooding with liquid. Jesus, no man had ever touched her and set her off like a Roman candle.

Jakob slid his tongue along the seam of her closed lips. Without hesitation, Lani opened her mouth. He stole inside. A moan of pleasure filled the room, and she realized it was her. Just from a kiss, from the feel of his invasion, and she was ready to come.

He tangled his hands in the neat chignon the hairdresser had created, destroying it. He wrenched his mouth away from hers, but before she could complain, he attacked her neck. Oh, hell, the man was very talented with this tongue and teeth. Primitive need pounded through her, urging her to get as close as possible. He kissed his way up to her ear, taking her sensitive lobe between his teeth.

"Jake."

Just that one little word had him pulling away from her. Cold air replaced the heat he had ignited.

"Sorry."

She blinked, her eyes opening to take in his expression. His face was flushed, his eyes heavy-lidded, and his hair was a wreck, which she was sure was her fault.

"Why are you apologizing?"

"I jumped the gun. I don't want to push you."

"You can push me as much as you want as long as it is down on the mattress."

He rolled his shoulders and opened his mouth to say something else stupid. She was sure, but Lani had had enough. The long months of working hard and losing a relationship with her brother...that all added up. But Jakob had said he wanted her. He had kissed her like his life depended on it. Now this?

She stepped closer and drew in a deep breath. The sweet, night air tangled with his masculine scent, leaving her more than a little lightheaded. Using her index finger, she trailed a path down his chest along the row of buttons of his dress shirt.

"I think I know what I want. I'm not underaged. In fact, I am well past the age of consent. It's not like I'm a virgin."

He drew in a deep breath, and she looked up at him.

"I don't want to hear about that."

"Only fair since I've seen things about you in the rag magazines for over a decade. And besides, please don't tell me you're one of those guys who expects a woman to stay pure."

"I'm not. I just—"

He broke off his words and looked away.

"You just?" Lani asked, using a light, teasing tone. It was hard to do because her heart was beating out of control. While she wasn't a virgin, she wasn't usually the one who seduced. It seemed Jakob forced her out of her comfort zone once again.

The heavy sigh filled the space between them, and she wondered if she had read him wrong.

That is until he answered her.

"I just don't like thinking about *you* with other men. Especially that asshole, Rick. I know it's not the right way to behave, but I need to punch him every time I see him."

She bit back a smile. "That's something we have in common, at least."

He chuckled, giving her the courage to rise up to her toes. Without hesitation, she pressed her mouth against his, crowding as close as she could to him. This time, she was the one who slipped her tongue between his lips. She moved her hands over his shoulders again as he slid his arms around her waist...then lower.

The next second, he took over the kiss, his mouth slanting

over hers. She didn't know how it could go from hot to a blazing five-alarm fire, but that's the way it was between them.

When he pulled away from her this time, he spun her around.

"This dress has got to go. Did I tell you that you look gorgeous in it? Well, you do, but it just...I need to feel your skin."

Lifting her hair, he put it over her shoulder so it was out of his way. She thought he would yank the zipper down from the way he had been talking, but instead, his slow, steady movements left her a mess. If she thought her nipples were hard before, she had been mistaken. She shifted her weight and felt the dampness of her panties.

He's barely touched me.

He kissed the back of her neck, tongue, lips... teeth. That little nip had her moaning.

"Oh, love, that's one of the most beautiful sounds I have ever heard."

She wanted to tell him he didn't have to say things like that. Little lies lovers told each other didn't need to be between them, but she wanted the fantasy. If she was truthful with herself, she'd been infatuated with him for a decade. So, for this one night, she wanted...no, she needed the fantasy he was creating.

He slid the zipper down, the backs of his fingers trailing down her spine, his mouth following along. She felt him fall to his knees behind her.

"Let it fall, and take off your bra."

Usually, she didn't like anyone telling her what to do, even in the bedroom. But when that lazy tone dissolved into an order...she shivered. The man was killing her with each comment, each kiss, each touch. Once she rid herself of her bra and dress, he slipped his fingers beneath the waistband of her panties and slid them down her legs.

"Fuck me, this ass. Do you know how many times I've wanted to touch you just because of this ass?"

She looked over her shoulder at him. Jakob was looking up at her like she was a goddess.

"How many times?"

His eyes seemed to darken. "Too many to count."

Then, he leaned forward to kiss first one cheek, then the other, his gaze never leaving hers. He bit one, and she gasped. It didn't hurt, but it sent another blast of longing racing through her blood.

Unexpectedly, he rose and turned her around to face him. Before she knew what was happening, she was flat on her back on the mattress.

She opened her mouth to insist he get naked, but she was left gasping once again when he dropped to his knees and yanked her forward. Her legs were dangling off the side of the bed.

He set a hand on each of her thighs, pressing them further apart.

"Yes," he growled. He reached out and looked up at her. "So wet, baby."

Oh, damn, the way he said baby...she could die happy now.

Again, without breaking eye contact, he leaned forward and licked her, his tongue slipping just a little inside of her sex.

"Heaven...fuck."

He closed his eyes and did it again, humming as he continued to lick her like she was his favorite treat. She didn't think she could get any more aroused until he slipped his finger inside of her, then took her clit between his teeth.

"Oh, damn."

She was lifting up against him as he tasted and teased her. Tension gathered in her stomach, then slipped lower. So close... then all of a sudden, she broke free as pleasure rolled through her, leaving her gasping for air and shouting his name at the same time.

"Beautiful."

He stood and started to pull off his clothes. She used the little bit of energy she had left to rise to her elbows and watch. She had seen a lot of pictures of him over the years. He had gone from a fit young adult to a solid man with sculpted muscles and broad shoulders. Her gaze slipped lower. Oh, wow. She guessed the rumors were accurate in that regard.

She licked her lips.

"You look so decadent right now."

It took some effort to raise her gaze to his again. "And don't worry. I'll have you on your knees soon, but right now, I want inside you. Move up."

She didn't have to be told more than once. He went to his nightstand and pulled out a condom. Tearing it open, he rolled it on with what looked to be shaking hands. Then he was pressing her into the mattress. He rose to his knees, then notched his dick at her entrance. His entry was swift, fast.

"Lani...fuck me..."

"I am," she said.

He looked down at her, his mouth twitching. "No. Well, yes, you are. It's just that all of the fantasies I've had for years didn't prepare me for just how amazing you are,"

He dropped his mouth to hers. Lani could taste herself on his tongue as she pulled it deeper into her mouth. Groaning, he lifted his head as he started to thrust. Each time he entered her, she felt her need build once again. She wasn't a woman who had multiple orgasms, and definitely not with a man or during sex.

But each time Jakob drove into her, the tension inched closer and closer to another explosion. He dipped his head to take one of her nipples into his mouth, sucking and nipping at the tip. She barely registered the sound of the headboard smacking against the wall as his rhythm increased.

He rose to his knees, dragging her up by her hips. Each powerful thrust pushed her closer and closer to the pinnacle, but it remained out of reach.

Jakob thrust deep, then held himself still inside of her. He pressed his fingers against her clit...once...twice...

"Come for me, baby. Let me feel all those muscles on my cock."

He pressed hard with his thumb, and she was falling into a million pieces, shouting his name once more.

With that, he started to move.

"Fuck, yes, so good."

He groaned her name as he followed her with one last hard plunge back into her.

A few moments later, he fell on top of her. Both of them were still breathing heavily. Lani's entire body was still sensitive when he finally roused himself to pull out of her.

"Sorry, I fell on you like an oaf."

"No worries, Jake."

"Be right back," he said, leaning down and giving her a quick kiss.

She felt cold without him on top of her.

So, all the gossip about Jake being a fantastic lover was not fiction. Her entire body was still vibrating with tiny little sparks of pleasure. He had been right. The years of fantasies were nothing compared to the real thing.

Now, she had to live in the moment because she knew that Jakob Wulf was a walking heartbreak. She just needed to enjoy him while she had him.

Jakob trashed the condom and paused to look at himself in the mirror. Even in the darkness, he could tell he didn't look any different, but he felt different. His entire world had shifted. He'd had plenty of good sex. Raunchy, fun...all kinds. But this was different.

Lani was different.

Pushing that aside, he returned to bed. She immediately rolled over and snuggled. Usually, he hated that. He had issues, but with Lani, it felt normal...perfect.

How did he keep her and not lose her because of her brother?

"What is happening there in your head?"

Her voice was sleepy. Her head was on his chest. In that instant, he knew he wanted this. Forever. Oh, Jesus, he had known he wanted a relationship with her, but he never prepared himself for that kind of thought.

He had never called a romantic partner love before now. Jakob knew precisely why. He was in love with her.

Lani lifted her head. The only light in the room was from the moon, but he had always had pretty good night vision. "What's wrong?"

He forced himself to relax, unable to reveal what he'd just realized. "Just…"

She sat up and pulled the sheet with her, hiding her magnificent breasts. Dammit. "You regret it, don't you?"

When he said nothing, she sighed and slipped out of bed. Panic set in, and he reacted, leaning forward and pulling her back into bed.

"Argh!" she said as he rolled them over the king mattress. Once he was on top of her, he settled an arm on each side of her head and looked down at her. Damn, she was beautiful. Her dark hair fanned out over the white sheets, and her eyes were in angry slits.

"Get off me. I want to go home."

"You can go home. But I want to clear something up first."

Her chin notched up. "Fine."

God, she was magnificent. He was always attracted to strong women. At the exact moment, though, he wanted to protect her, physically and emotionally. He needed her to know there was more to this thing between them.

"I do not regret anything about tonight. Well, no. I do regret having to dance with that vapid friend of Royal's. But I do not regret anything that's happened between us. In fact, I hope to do that again very soon."

"Then what are you worrying about?"

"It's…well, guys don't take their best friend's little sister to bed."

"That's stupid."

"Well, it's a code."

"It's an asinine code."

Lani's voice had taken on a condescending tone. He laughed. Her frown seemed to lessen, and her eyes lit up.

"I love your laugh."

"Right back at ya, love."

"You don't have to worry about Ben."

"That's easier said than done."

"No, it's not. I'm an adult. He didn't have a problem with Rick and me."

"Don't talk about other men while you're lying beneath me naked, and I'm hard as a rock."

"And what are we going to do about that, Jake?"

Jakob thought he couldn't get any harder. He had been wrong. The moment he heard her teasing words in that seductive tone...well, he was lucky he didn't come in his pants. He knew that he shouldn't be doing what he was doing, but as she leaned up to take his bottom lip into her mouth to suck on it... Jesus. Every thought of being a good guy disintegrated and was replaced with need. He wanted to touch her, taste her, and he wanted that all to happen immediately. Again and again.

He rolled off her and slipped off the bed.

"Jake—"

He slipped his arms beneath her and lifted her off the mattress. "I think we need a shower."

"Is that your way of telling me that I stink?"

She was smiling at him, and that was all he cared about. Screw his best friend. Ben would need to learn that his love for Lani was real.

Love. Yep, he wasn't even freaking out thinking he was in love with her. But he knew she wasn't ready to hear those words from him. Not yet.

He stopped by the light switch. "Can you get the lights?"

She flipped the switch, and he made his way to the counter. After setting her down, he headed to the shower. He turned it on then faced Lani. Her gaze had been down where his ass was, and he smiled. Her eyes widened.

"Yeah, that always happens when I'm around you."

"It does not."

"Eyes up here," he said, amusement filling his voice.

Her cheeks were stained red when she finally looked up.

"And yes, it does. It has for years. I'd see you, and I'd get hard. Why did you think I'd been avoiding you?"

"Lack of taste?"

He barked out and laughed. "God, that is why I'll always want you. You give me shit every chance you get. Well, and the fact that you are the most beautiful woman I have ever seen."

She rolled her eyes. "You don't have to seduce me."

"Yeah," he said, leaning forward, pulling her bottom lip into his mouth just as she had done to his. He let it go. "You deserved to be romanced every moment of your life, Lani."

And he planned on doing just that for the rest of their lives. He just planned on waiting to inform her because she might freak out and run in the other direction.

"Now," he said, lifting her off the counter and into his arms, "I think we should see what fun we can get up to in the shower."

He had spent the better part of the last hour looking for Lani. She seemed to have disappeared. As he hurried down the hall, he knew there would be hell to pay.

"Lose something?"

He stopped in his tracks and glanced at the open doorway. It was the conference room. His partner motioned him in.

"What the hell happened?"

"She's disappeared."

A roll of his partner's eyes told him all he needed to know. "People don't disappear."

"Yes, they do."

The anger on his partner's face had him worried. "Have you noticed that the movie star disappeared too?"

He rolled his shoulders as irritation slinked down his spine. "No."

"No? Do you mean that you hadn't noticed or that they aren't together?"

"I'm sure they aren't together. In fact, she hates him."

"Tsk, tsk. That's odd that you're ignoring that they have been seen together since he arrived. We might have a problem."

"I heard her say more than once that the guy pissed her off."

Pity moved over his partner's expression. "We don't have time for you to be this stupid. I would guess that the two of them are fucking or will be later. He was watching her all night."

Something cold settled in his stomach.

"If you had done your job, this wouldn't be a problem. Get your shit together, or I'll find someone else to help me with this and share the money with him."

With that decree, his partner turned and strode away from him. Not for the first time, he thought that if he had just walked away from the deal...to try to have an everyday life without all the plans and idiocy, he might have been happy. He could have explained it all to Lani, and she would have understood.

Now, though, he was probably damned to hell.

Eleven

"Why don't you blow your brother off?"

Lani shook her head as she smiled at Jakob. How did this man look so good in the morning? Maybe he didn't. Perhaps he had just dissolved all of her brain cells with the four times...yes, *four*...he'd made love to her. "I told you, I promised that I would be there. You could come with me."

"I'm not up for pretending."

They both had agreed it would be best to keep what was happening between them a secret. They didn't even know if they would last.

"Wait, isn't that sort of your job?"

He shrugged as he pulled on his dress shirt from the night before. The man was so, so pretty. She had known he was. Hell, his image is splashed all over the place when he has a movie release. He didn't just have a six-pack. It was eight or more. She hadn't been able to keep her hands off him the night before.

She had never been like that. *Ever.* There was just something about Jakob. When she touched him, everything else seemed to fade.

"It is, but the truth is, I've wanted you for too long. If I'm around your brother, then he'll know."

He took her hand and threaded his fingers through hers. It was odd but also kind of weirdly romantic. Not that many guys had tried to romance her. Not with sweet gestures like this.

"And that would be a problem?"

"Not for me. Probably for Ben."

They stopped by the door where their shoes sat. He pulled their joined hands up so he could kiss her hand. Again, romantic and a little...oh, who was she kidding? The old-fashioned gesture had her heart galloping and her entire body lighting up.

"Ah, is this a stupid guy thing?"

"No comment."

She rolled her eyes.

"So, you don't want to come with me to brunch or whatever this idiocy is? But you want to spend the day together?"

"Yeah. I'll wait here, and then we can spend the day together. I need to make a few calls, mainly to my sister. I must let her know it will be another day or two until I make it to Maui. You should come with me."

Something warm moved through her. "I'd like that a lot."

After the door shut behind Lani, Jakob made another cup of coffee and moved out to the lanai. It was still early, but not too early for people to hit the beach. He enjoyed this time of day in Hawai'i, where everything seemed to awaken and explode simultaneously. The air was always dewy and sweet in the morning, and while things could suck even if you lived in Hawai'i, at least it was beautiful.

His phone buzzed in his pocket, and he pulled it out. It was his sister.

"Hey, how are you doing?"

"Jakob."

It wasn't his sister. Instead, it was Alek. He sounded as if he'd aged fifty years since the last time they'd chatted.

"What's wrong?" he asked, alarm racing through him.

"I'm not sure. I had to bring your sister to the ER. She started having contractions about an hour ago. They are doing all sorts of tests, but she wanted me to call you. The doctor said it shouldn't be too serious, even if she goes into labor. She's far enough along that we should be out of the woods. But...she's scared, and I told her I would get her anything to make her feel better. She wants you over here."

"Of course," he said, already making his way indoors. "I was going to wait until tomorrow to fly over. I had Felix on standby today. I'll call him and be over there as soon as I can. Have you talked to Mother or Jensen?"

"No. She wants to wait since they can't make it over here as easily. She wants to ensure she has some answers for them."

"Got it. I'll text you once we have a take-off time."

"Thanks, Jake."

He hung up just as the front door opened. Marta stepped in.

"Marta, what are you doing here? You don't work on Sundays."

"I thought I would stop by. You said maybe you were going to Maui."

"I wasn't, but now I have to. Jules is in the hospital."

Alarm had her eyes widening.

"She's far enough along, but they are doing tests to ensure everything is okay. I'm going to get dressed and head out." He hurried to the stairs and realized he had no way to the airport. "Damn. Can you drop me off at the airport?"

"Of course, Jakob. Go get your things. Do you need me to contact Felix?"

"Yes, thanks."

He headed up the stairs and tried calling Lani.

"Aloha, this is Lani. I can't answer my phone right now, but leave a message, and I'll get back to you."

Damn. "Lani, I have to head out to Maui. Jules is in labor or having contractions or something. If I don't hear back from you before we take off, I'll call you once we land, or I'll use the communications on the plane. I...I hate leaving like this." He sighed. "I already miss you."

He hung up before he started to beg her to understand why he had to leave. He knew Lani would understand; he felt unsettled about not talking to her. Pushing those feelings aside, he started to fill a suitcase. After changing clothes, he grabbed his toiletries. He followed Marta out the door within ten minutes of hanging up with Alek.

He just prayed everything was okay with Jules and the baby.

Lani pulled into the parking garage down the street from the brunch location her brother had texted her earlier. It was a busy Sunday morning, so she'd had to park on the top level. When she grabbed her purse, she checked her phone. She smiled when she saw there was a voicemail from Jakob. The smile faded as soon as she heard the fear in Jakob's voice. It had been thirty minutes since he'd left the message. She tried calling him, but it went to voicemail. She frowned.

"Jake, call me when you land. Don't worry about getting hold of me. Jules comes first. I already miss you, too."

She clicked her phone off. Worry for Jules and her baby made her stomach ache. When she had seen Jakob's sister a couple of months ago, she was glowing. Her joy had made Lani a little envious, but she had been happy for her, too.

There was another part of her, a small, petty part of her, that felt cheated. It wasn't important, but after a decade of being infatuated with Jakob, she finally had him in bed...and in the shower...and now she had to wait for more. But what was it that her mother used to say? Anticipation makes things sweeter.

Sighing, she slipped her phone into her pocket and headed for the stairs.

When Lani stepped out of the building, she slipped on her sunglasses and started the three-block walk to the restaurant her sister-in-law had picked. She couldn't wait to get her car back. It had been over a week. Today was one of those perfect Oahu days, with just enough trade winds to keep cool. She would prefer to have the wind whipping through her hair.

She had thought it odd that Ben hadn't wanted Jakob at the brunch. It was also weird that they were having it in Honolulu. There was a good chance that someone would recognize one of them, but maybe that was Royal's idea. Yep, it had to be Royal's plan all along. At least she would get some food out of it. She had definitely worked up an appetite the night before.

Still, it had been odd that Ben hadn't said anything to Jakob about it. From what Jakob said, though, they had barely spoken. Ben had been off for a couple of years. It wasn't until he'd started dating Royal that it really hit her that he wasn't the boy she grew up with. Hell, he wasn't even the man he had grown into. And she never understood his infatuation with Royal. In fact, he had been getting bored with her, or at least that is what Lani thought, right before he announced their engagement.

Even after that, she was sure he would call it off. He looked like he'd checked out of the relationship more than once. Her brother would never cheat. That wasn't his style, but he had been getting antsy up until about six weeks ago.

She'd reached the second-floor landing when her phone pinged. She pulled it out and frowned. It was a text from her brother.

Ben: *Not gonna make it today.*

She frowned. That wasn't the way he usually wrote texts. It sounded off. But then, maybe he was still hung over from the night before. He had been drinking a lot of champagne, and that always made him feel like crap the next day.

Lani: *Okay. No worries.*

She slipped her phone into her pocket. Why did he wait until five minutes before they were supposed to meet to text her? Royal and Ben were coming all the way over from Turtle Bay. It seemed like he would have known before now.

With Jakob on his way off the island, she was at odds with what to do. She could head back to her apartment and get comfortable. She had been resentful when Royal had said she wanted to have brunch today, but when she said it had been Ben's idea, Lani knew it was important.

She made her way back up the stairs. As she stepped into the parking area, she heard a squeal of tires. Alarm lit through her as she turned to see a car barreling toward her. She started to run, trying to get out of the path of the SUV that was now seemingly headed straight for her. Knowing that it would hit her before she could actually get away, she took a chance and jumped in between two cars, her hip crashing into the car on her right. She landed with a thud, pain exploding in her knee as she fell forward. Her hands slipped over the pavement as she tried to keep from having her face smash into the pavement. As it was, her cheek hit, and she knew it was scraped up.

"Miss? Miss?"

The sound of feet running toward her reached her. A young woman and what looked to be her mother came rushing toward her.

"Are you okay?" The older woman asked.

Lani rose, her head spinning a little. "Yeah. I think so."

"It was like that man was aiming for you," the young woman said, reaching out to help Lani.

"Mahalo," she said. "I think it might have been some people just being jerks."

The women shared a look, and she could tell when they turned toward her that they weren't convinced.

"Thank you again."

"Do you want us to call the police?" The mother asked.

"N-no. I...I just need to get checked out."

They looked like they wanted to argue, but she felt unsafe there. And she didn't want the women to be exposed if the jerk returned.

"Thanks," she said, rushing off. She got to her SUV before she felt her eyes start to sting. Someone had just tried to kill her, run her down. Lani knew not everyone loved her, but to want to kill her? That was another level.

And that's precisely what it was. Now the failed brakes, the weird text she had gotten...the feeling that someone was watching her...it all seemed to add up. She might be blowing it out of proportion, and since she couldn't call Jakob, she knew there was one other man she could call.

She pulled out her phone, found his number, and clicked on it.

"Hey," Conner Dillon said, "Please tell me you aren't calling to reschedule."

She sighed. "No. I need to talk to you about a personal security issue."

"Are you safe right now?" he asked, his teasing tone dissolving.

"I think. I just..."

She was ready to start crying, which wasn't like her at all.

"Are you in Honolulu?"

"Yes."

"Go to my office. I'll let security know to let you in. They will stay with you until I get there."

"I'm sorry to bother you on a Sunday."

"Don't worry about that. Just get to my office. We'll take care of everything else."

Emily Daniels burst out of the elevator and hurried down the hall, dread growing with each step she took. Dillon Security was deathly silent as she made her way to Conner Dillon's office. It was Sunday morning, so that made sense. What didn't make sense was the big man calling her in. Conner didn't expect his folks to work on the weekend unless they were on a job that required it.

As she entered his outer office, Janet wasn't in her seat. His personal assistant was usually his right hand. She raised her hand and realized it was shaking. In a deep breath, Emily reminded herself that her brothers were okay. Aaron was visiting their parents. The twins, Baxter and Barrett, were deployed, but she assumed her parents would call her before Conner would know.

She knocked and waited for Conner to respond.

"Come in, Emily."

She took another deep breath and opened the door. Conner was leaning against his big desk. In his early forties, her boss was a hottie. Lean and muscular, the former FBI agent was definitely dreamy. The fact that he was a dedicated father with two kids and insanely in love with his wife added to the appeal. He wore jeans and a button-down shirt, the sleeves rolled up.

"Hey, boss."

His brow furrowed. "Why do you look like that?"

She would not shift her weight. She knew that was a tell with her. "Like what?"

"Like you're about to be fired."

"I'm worried about why you would call me in on a Sunday afternoon."

It took a second, but his eyes widened. "Oh, sorry. The brothers are fine, as far as I know. Or as fine as your family can be."

She released a breath she didn't know she had been holding. It was then she realized there was another person in the room. Turning, her eyes widened.

A young woman sat on the comfy couch Conner kept in his office. With golden eyes and long dark hair, Hawaiian wore a pair of shorts and a t-shirt with the Kingston Surfing logo on it. Emily took in her appearance and the bandage on her right knee. There was also a scrape on her right cheek.

"Lani Kingston, how the heck are you?"

"I've been better," she said, her lyrical voice filled with trepidation.

"You two know each other?"

She glanced over at Conner. "Yeah. The one year I went to school here." Before the Marines decided to move them. Again.

"This might work better than I thought."

She turned to look at her boss. "What might work?"

"Ms. Kingston has come to us for protection. I would like you to be that protection."

That explained the bandaged knee. "I feel there is a but coming."

"Ms. Kingston?"

It wasn't normal for the boss to cede the explanation of any job, but he apparently knew Lani just needed some kind of control.

"Please, call me Lani."

Her gaze moved to Emily, and memories came flooding back to her. Emily had always been awkward—still was—but being a military kid made each move extremely difficult. Lani had been sweet to Emily.

"I've had some situations in the last three weeks."

"And what would those incidents be? No, first tell me about this morning."

"You know?"

"Lani," she said, softening her voice because the other woman seemed fragile, "your knee is bandaged."

She sighed. "Oh, yeah. Sorry."

"You have nothing to be sorry for, Lani. Just tell me what happened this morning. Wait...didn't your brother just get married yesterday?"

Lani nodded. Emily remembered reading how big it was going to be. The bride had been an influencer and used it to push her social media reach. True love, for sure.

"Yes. I was almost run over in a parking garage."

"And you had other incidences?"

"One other for sure. The brakes in my car went out. And I've felt like someone has been watching me for the last few weeks. I thought it was stress, but now I wonder."

Anger swelled in Emily. No one should be terrorized this way. But the fact that she was in their office without anyone by her side was telling.

"You don't trust your family."

Sadness settled on Lani's expression. She was far from the happy, sweet girl who had been nice to Emily.

"No." Shame threaded her whispered response.

Oh, damn. Lani had one brother, Ben, but Emily knew the Kingston extended family was huge. She probably had over fifty people who would want to kill her for the money.

"Okay." She looked at Conner. "Why do we need to pretend I'm not her protection?"

Conner's eyebrows shot up in surprise. "How did you know?"

"You said it would be good that we knew each other."

He nodded. "Ms. Kingston doesn't want anyone to know about the attempts."

Emily's gaze moved back to Lani. "You have no idea who it might be?"

Lani shook her head. Emily's heart ached for the other woman. She seemed to be lost. She looked over at her boss.

"You knew about them though?"

Conner shook his head. "No. I've been chatting with Lani about coming to work for us."

"Do you mind if I used the restroom?" Lani asked.

Conner shook his head. "It's just outside the office on the opposite side of the hall from us."

Lani nodded and rose. Her gaze took in Emily. "I hope you can be my protector. I trust you."

Emily nodded. She watched the other woman as she walked out of the room. She moved gracefully as if she were a princess heading to the palace. Rumors were that the Kingstons were related to the Hawaiian royal family, and it showed in her poise. Emily turned to her boss.

"So, what's the plan, boss?"

Conner always had a plan. He probably had a plan of all his plans.

"You are going to move in with her. She's going to start working for us."

That had Emily blinking. "Wait, doesn't she work for Kingston?"

"She did. Or I guess she is about to send in her resignation. I've been trying to poach her for months. So, we'll lead with that idea. She'll put it out there that she's in our Miami office. She truly has no idea who this could be, and since they have tried twice in less than a month, there's a good chance they will try again soon. Since most people think you're admin, it would make sense that you were her executive assistant."

It was a role she had played a lot, and it always worked. Most of the time, she went into a company to ferret out embezzlers or people selling company secrets.

"You okay with a new assignment?"

She nodded. "I finished that hotel job last week, and my reports have been filed."

It was what she did a lot. She went in to find out who was embezzling from one of the hotel restaurants. It hadn't been that hard to figure out which person in management had sticky fingers.

"We're actually going to put out that she is in Miami. I've already talked to my sister about it."

Conner's sister ran the Miami office, which was their headquarters.

"You don't trust her family?"

He shook his head. "If anything happens to her brother, she gets everything. And it's reciprocated."

Emily whistled. "Gotcha. Millionaire, at least, and many greedy people would want her out of the way."

"Yes. She explained more about how the company would be distributed, so I will have people start digging here. I'll have you stay at the Tree Top House."

It wasn't a house on top of a tree but high up and out in the middle of nowhere. It was completely off-grid, so it was easy to hide people there. The ownership papers would only lead to an LLC not affiliated with Dillon Security.

As soon as she heard Lani's soft steps, she turned. "So, I'm gonna be your assistant. I guess we're taking off today?"

Lani's expression turned even sadder. "Yes. And I don't have to quit."

"That was the plan," Conner said. Only someone who knew him as well as Emily would see the eye twitch. He did not like changing plans.

"Well, my brother just fired me via text."

TWELVE

J akob looked at his mobile for the third time in the last ten minutes.

"You should call her."

"I did when I landed."

"But it had gone to voicemail."

He looked at his sister. Other than looking a little tired, she was fine. She'd had false labor, and usually, they would have sent her home. Unfortunately, her blood pressure was too high, so her doctor insisted she stay at the hospital.

"How did you know?"

She offered him a tired smile. "Come tell me what happened yesterday. How was the wedding? I saw some pics online. None of you, besides the one she posted of the wedding party."

He knew who the *she* was. Royal. There was no doubt his sister hadn't changed her mind about the other woman. But there were more important things than his love life.

"I don't want to bother you."

She shook her head. "I need some kind of distraction."

He sat in the chair beside the bed and took her offered hand. "I slipped out early."

"Oh, yeah. And what did you do? Please tell me you did something other than go to bed."

He smiled. "I took Lani out to eat."

"Wait, didn't she have a full three-course meal at the reception? I saw the Instagram pics from Royal's maid of honor."

"No. Too many relatives brought in extras, and there wasn't enough. So, I took her out to eat at Zippy's."

"Oh...you had a date. Tell me you were both dressed up when you went in."

"We were. It's that prom experience all the Americans talk about, you know. Going out to eat at a fast-food place in formal wear. It was odd, but no one bothered us. I mean, she's a celebrity of sorts, but...it was nice."

"Yes. It's one of the things I love about Hawai'i. Locals pay attention, but they often don't intrude. It's nice. Please tell me you closed the deal."

He opened his mouth to answer, but Jules was in a mood for obvious reasons. "Did you have problems closing the deal? I can have Alek talk to you. Or better yet, I'll get Jensen on the line too and they can explain just how to satisfy a woman."

His sister. It was his damned fault that she could be so plain-spoken. "I didn't have problems closing the deal."

"Oh, my. That sounds promising."

He rolled his eyes. "She left this morning to have brunch with Royal and her brother."

"You weren't invited?"

"No, and I didn't want to chance Ben realizing what had happened."

"Jakob, what the hell? You don't want to shout from the rooftops that she's your woman?"

With every fiber of his being.

"Yes, I do. But I promised Ben I wouldn't mess with her."

"Recently?"

"When I first met her."

She studied him for a long moment. As he'd always thought, she was the youngest but probably the smartest. Jules thought things through. It made her dangerous when she was younger. The youngest Wulf liked exacting revenge, but usually days or weeks after an altercation.

"She was underaged, Jake. He didn't want you bugging his sister then. Was she always pretty?"

He nodded.

"And there were probably a lot of surfers they sponsored who were hitting on her. You were more well-known than any of those idiots. Add in your accent...Americans love a British accent. They find it hard to resist."

"I concur," Alek said from behind Jakob. He turned and found his brother-in-law leaning against the doorjamb. Alek wasn't looking at him, though. His gaze was taking in Jules.

"Love, come tell Jake he's being an idiot."

"I will not," he said, but he still walked into the room and around to the other side of the bed. He sat on the mattress. "Guys have a code."

"It's an idiot code. She is a grown woman. It's not like she's sixteen anymore."

He shared a look with Alek. Jakob had threatened his brother-in-law the first time he'd met him. That was until he saw the way Alek gazed at Jules. There was no doubt Alek was in love with her.

"Good God, you just have to admit you love her. Then everything will be okay."

His gaze narrowed. "Excuse me?"

She looked at her husband. "When he gets prissy, he's been found out. He already knows he loves her but is afraid to admit it to her."

Like he said, the smartest of the family.

"I have a feeling if I professed my love to her after one night, she wouldn't take it seriously."

"This isn't a one-night stand you picked up. This is a woman you have known for a decade."

"Calm down, love," Alek said in his deep, calm voice. "I think your brother has a plan, and you don't need to get all riled up about it."

She sighed and muttered something that sounded like *idiot* under her breath.

"Fine. You should go back to Oahu."

"No. I'm on orders to stay here. Besides, I'm sending the jet back to England."

"Why?"

"Mother is coming. You know she couldn't fly commercial. I could, but I promised her I would stay with you until she arrived."

For a second, she looked irritated, then...relieved. When he talked to Nic, she told him Jules would want her mother there. As usual, Nic was right.

"I'm going to let you get some rest." He stood and kissed her forehead. "Take it easy, Jules. You and that little one are more important than any work."

"Love you."

"Love you."

"I'll see you out," Alek said, giving Jules a pat on the hand. Once they were in the hallway and the door closed, Alek blew out a sigh of relief. "Thanks for coming. She insisted on going home, and I would rather she stay here, as her doctor said. And for getting your mom ready because that is one thing I knew she needed, but she didn't want to bother your mother."

They both shook their heads. They were a close family, and there was no way that his mother wouldn't hop on a plane.

"I didn't tell her that the entire family is coming over. I thought she would freak out a little."

"Everyone?"

He nodded. "When there's an important event like this, we like to gather."

"Yeah, I've noticed."

"Where is my grandson!" A voice bellowed down the hall.

"Damn, I should have called him later."

A tall Hawaiian turned the corner the next instant, and his gaze zeroed in on Alek.

"Aleka," he said.

Alek's grandfather looked so much like him. His hair was salt and pepper and longer than Alek's. His brother-in-law tended to keep his shorter. All those years in the military probably made it hard to want longer hair. But the eyes...those were the same shape and color.

"Tutu, everything is fine. False labor."

"Then why is she still here?"

"Her blood pressure is too high. They want to keep an eye on her."

"You should let her rest. Why are you not treating her better?"

Jakob chuckled, which earned a frown from Alek's grandfather. "Sorry, but you and I know he would do anything for my sister. She's hardheaded."

His expression lightened slightly. "True. It's one of the things I like best about her."

"Go on in. She will be happy to see you. I need to give Jake the security codes for the house."

"Got it. Good to see you, Jake."

"Tutu!" Jules exclaimed. Once the door shut behind his grandfather, Alek sighed again.

"I figured it would be better to have him here to fight her. I can to a point, but they are both hardheaded and, well, he'll guilt her."

Jakob nodded.

He gave Jakob the codes. "It's the day I met your sister for the first time."

"Who would have thought such a tough Army Ranger would go all soft and romantic."

"I think you're about to find out. Mark my words. Once you realize how important a woman is to you, you will burn down the whole world if it means keeping her safe."

Alek slapped him on the back, then returned to the room. Jakob made his way down the hall. He heard a few whispers but wasn't sure anyone recognized him. Instead, he assumed it had more to do with being a hospital.

Once outside, he tried calling Lani again but only got her voicemail.

"Love, you're worrying me. Please let me know if everything is okay. I'm sending the jet back for Mother, and I promised I would stay here until she landed, but she would understand if you needed me."

He headed to his rental car with a hollow pit in his stomach.

He knew everything was probably okay, but something didn't sit right with him.

Jakob drove down the hallway to Conner Dillon's office four days later. He ignored the young woman at the desk in the outer office and burst into Conner's office. He was sitting behind his desk, not looking at all surprised about the intrusion.

"Come on in, Wulf. Good of you to visit."

"Fuck off. Where is she?"

"I had no idea he was so hot-headed," a cultured British voice said.

That's when Jakob noticed a tall, dark-haired man standing by the windows. He wore dress pants, shiny shoes, and a tie with his dress shirt. Jakob would still know he wasn't local just by the outfit if he hadn't spoken. He said nothing to the man and turned his attention back to Conner. He was still sitting behind his desk, studying him.

"Mr. Dillon, I'm sorry," his admin said from behind him.

"Don't worry, Clarice. I was expecting him. Close the door behind you."

He said nothing until the door closed. "You were expecting me?"

"Yes. We've been keeping an eye on your movements."

"Where. Is. Lani?" He bit out each word.

"She's safe."

He opened his mouth to say something else, but then the words registered. "What do you mean she's safe?"

"He means that the person who tried to run her down didn't succeed." That came from the Brit.

That one sentence had his heart almost stopping.

"Jesus, Mix, don't be so blunt. He looks like he's going to pass out."

"Don't call me Mix. My name's—"

"Ian."

He glanced at Jakob, then back to his boss. "Someone has been leaking information."

"Your sister says hi."

He blinked. "Autumn sent you? How do you know her?"

"He's going to lead the new show and met with TFH today." Jakob looked at Dillon, who shrugged. "I told you we were keeping track of your movements. And I let Autumn know she could tell you. You checked out."

Jakob had wanted to skip the meeting, but the production company had been adamant. Once the TFH team member told him to talk to Dillon, he finished up as fast as possible and headed to Dillon Security.

"Go back to the fact that she was almost run over. When the fuck did that happen, and why didn't anyone contact me?"

"We had to check you out. Lani insisted that you would never do anything like that, but I don't know you personally."

Their family had hired them for security a time or two, but they did not know each other.

"You've only been on the island for twelve hours, so I'm impressed."

"My sister's in the hospital, but you know that."

He nodded.

"I was going to hire a PI until Autumn told me about you."

"Well, Ian will take you to her safe house, but I want to

discuss what has happened since you left. You might want to take a seat."

Lani sipped her tea as she gazed out at the trees below, feeling trapped. When they first arrived at the safe house, she had been elated. It was off the beaten path, tucked away in the forest. Each morning, Birds singing just outside her window woke her. She spent her days in the gardens down below. It was on the third day that she started to get antsy.

Now that she was on the fourth day of confinement, she was ready to scream. She didn't have her phone. They had taken it from her when she'd started getting nasty texts and DMs. They all seemed to come from the same person—they could not track.

She wanted to talk to Jakob. She needed to hear his voice. How had she gone from being annoyed by him to needing him after one night in his bed?

"Stop looking so depressed," Emily said as she stepped out on the lanai.

Lani glanced at her protector. Emily was just as quirky as she remembered, with an irreverent sense of humor and a colorful vocabulary.

"I'm not depressed. I'm annoyed."

"Not at me, because I'm your bestie."

Lani's mouth curved. Yeah, it had only been a few days, but they had clicked. Maybe it was the yin and yang of their personalities.

"Just at the situation. Also, at the person pulling this crap."

Emily nodded. "I get it. I totally do. I would hate to be confined."

"You've been stuck here with me."

"It's my job, plus that last job was a pain. The number of tourists who think they can grab ass with the help is astounding. Getting a break from men is kind of nice."

She took the seat next to Lani at the little table.

"You act like Aaron isn't a man."

"Aaron is my brother, so he doesn't count. We aren't from Arkansas."

Lani snorted just as Aaron—known as Mad Dog from his days as an MMA fighter—stepped out on the lanai.

"He's here. And Mix is with him, so be nice."

Then he was gone. If Emily was loud and hilarious, Aaron was quiet and stoic.

"Is Conner coming?"

"Naw. It's someone you want to see."

"Who?"

"*Hollywood* is on his way up the drive."

Her heart leaped, then plummeted down into her stomach.

"Don't look like that. I have it on good authority that Hollywood stormed into Conner Dillon's office and read him the Riot Act. That man is hot to see you."

She heard the front doorbell chime.

"And he's here. Let's go see him."

Emily popped out of her chair. It took a second for Lani to react. He was finally here. Her world was tilting back another way, and she didn't know how to feel about it.

"Are you coming?" Emily called out.

"Yes," she said, practically jumping out of her chair and

hurrying to the door. No matter what, she wanted to see Jakob, even if it was to say goodbye if he didn't want the baggage that came with her.

THIRTEEN

J akob followed Ian Smith, Mix as he was known to everyone at TFH, up the massive steps. They had driven around for a few hours. Ian wanted to ensure that no one followed them to the estate. While they had state-of-the-art security, from the five cameras they'd passed on their way up the hill and the at least ten they'd passed after coming through the gate, Jakob knew this was one heavily protected home. With each security measure he spied on, he felt relieved and terrified. Relieved because she was so well-protected. Terrified that a man like Conner Dillon thought she needed this much protection.

The house was Asian in design, looking like something out of a movie, with two massive red doors.

"What's taking her so long?" Ian muttered as he leaned on the doorbell again.

"Who is it?" A singsongy voice said.

"Emily, open up."

"Say the password."

He rolled his eyes. "Is Aaron around?"

"Fine. That's not the password, by the way." Then, three

locks disengaged before the massive door opened. A tall, dark-haired woman stood on the other side. She had her hair up in a sloppy bun on top of her head. She smirked at both of them, but her crystal blue eyes were shrewd as she studied Jakob.

"Mix, what up?"

"Stop calling me that."

"It's your nickname."

"It isn't. It's a stupid name you came up with, and I don't like it."

The woman gasped dramatically. "My feelings are hurt."

He was barely paying attention to the byplay because Lani had just stepped into view.

His head had been filled with a discordant hum since he'd learned about her situation. Anger and fear had left his belly in a tight coil from the moment Conner Dillon had calmly told him someone had been trying to kill Lani. Now, she was here, and the spinning seemed to slow, and everything brightened.

She was...stunning. He didn't think he would ever think any differently. The white and blue Hawaiian print dress was loose, showing some cleavage and only hinting at her curves. Her hair was loose around her shoulders.

"Jake."

Just that one word, said in a breathy voice...and he was shoving the other two aside to get to her. He pulled her into his arms and slammed his mouth down on hers. She was here, safe, and nothing had happened to her.

The clearing of a throat brought him back from the brink. When Jacob lifted his head, they were both breathing heavily.

"Well, that was hot," the other woman said.

"Em," another male voice said. When he glanced over, he saw a man who looked vaguely familiar to Jakob. He had about two inches on Jakob and looked like he could pound Jakob into the ground. The other man reminded Jakob of his brother-in-law.

"It *was*. We can all admit it. Mix is just a spoilsport."

"Get bent, Emily," Ian said.

She laughed. "Come on, boys. We need to leave these two alone." She glanced at Jakob and winked. "All kinds of sound-proofing in this house."

As she led the two men away, Jakob said, "That big guy looks familiar."

"Mad Dog Daniels."

He glanced down at Lani. "What?"

"Mad Dog Daniels. MMA fighter or he was. He's also Emily's brother."

And, yeah, he saw it now. They had different coloring, but they had the same shade of eyes.

He took Lani's hand. "Your room?"

She smiled and started off toward the right of the entrance. He glanced back at the door and realized it was closed and locked. He hadn't even heard that happen. All that mattered was Lani.

By the time they reached her room, his entire body was buzzing. That happened around her all the time, but this was the first time seeing Lani since their night together. He knew how she would taste...how it sounded when she came.

He was happy he hadn't embarrassed himself and was lucky to be wearing jeans. Sure, he might have the imprint of his zipper on his dick, but at least it was keeping him in check, well, at least a little bit. He knew they should discuss what she had been going through, but hearing it from Dillon sent his protective instincts racing in front of his sane thoughts. There was a primitive need to touch, taste, and make her understand. She was his. Always.

"I like that dress."

She offered him a tremulous smile.

"You might want to take it off, though."

Cocking her head to one side, she studied him. "Why?"

This woman. "Because in the next five seconds, I'm going to tear it off your body."

He grabbed the bottom of his t-shirt, yanked it off, and threw it behind him.

Her tongue slipped out and wet her bottom lip as her gaze traveled down his body.

"Lani," he ground out.

She made eye contact again, a quirk of her lips, and he was worried. Stepping forward, her hands went to the waistband of his jeans.

"You didn't let me do everything I wanted last time."

She slipped a finger beneath the fabric of his pants and teased the head of his penis. Jesus.

"Tsk, tsk, not wearing any underwear."

He opened his mouth to respond to her taunt, but she leaned forward and pressed a kiss against his chest. Easily, she undid the button, then the zipper on his jeans before stepping back. Her eyes were dark, her face flushed, and he wanted inside her as soon as possible.

"Na-ah-ah, Jake. I get to do things to you. Things I've been dreaming about for a while. Drop those pants."

She lifted her chin and stared him down. She was magnificent. He didn't hesitate. He did as she ordered.

The curving of her mouth sent another wave of need spiraling through him. Her tongue swiped out again. Without another word, she slipped out of her dress, tossing it behind her. She wasn't wearing a bra. Fuck, she had the prettiest breasts he'd ever laid eyes on. All she wore was a minuscule pair of blue panties.

He reached out as she walked back to him, making her pause.

"No touching. You do that, and I can't think. I want to do this." She raised her gaze from his hand. "I need to do this."

He would give her anything she ever needed, so if she needed to torture him, he would allow it. Jakob dropped his hands to his sides. With a look of approval, she walked back to him and then fell to her knees in front of him. Her bent head was erotic enough for him to come, but the moment she wrapped her hand around his cock, he groaned.

"Oh, fuck, yes, that feels good," he muttered as she stroked him a few times. Then, he felt the flick of her tongue right before she took him fully into her mouth. Again and again, she took him into her mouth, deeper and deeper...and soon, he knew he would lose it if he didn't pull back.

"No!" She complained, but Jakob was pulling her up.

"I would be more than happy to let you do that until I come, but I need to be inside of you this time."

Her gaze ping-ponged back and forth, taking in his expression. She nodded as he bent his head to brush his mouth over hers. He walked her back to the mattress, then lifted her to toss her onto the bed. Her surprised gasp and laugh filled him with a sense of rightness. He wanted to spend the rest of his days making sure that she had more than enough reasons to laugh.

He grabbed hold of her panties. "These are sexy, but..." He ripped them off her body, tossed them behind him, and joined her on the bed.

Settling his arms on either side of her head, he looked down at her. The sweet smile she was giving him had his heart turning over. No one looking at that expression would assume she had done such dirty things with that mouth. Jakob wanted to tell her everything he felt but pulled back from that thought. So much was going on right now.

Leaning down, he acted as if he were close to kissing her mouth. At the last moment, he deviated to her neck. The squeal had his heart thumping hard against his chest. He kissed his way down her body, teasing her with his hands, mouth, tongue, and his teeth. He settled between her legs and wasted no time. Slipping his tongue between her pussy lips, he felt as if he were tasting heaven once more. She was sweet and salty and everything in between. And wet. She was so fucking wet.

By the time he pushed her up and over into an orgasm, his entire body was shaking with need. He crawled back up her body, dragging her hips up as he rose to his knees. He entered her in one hard thrust.

Her moan of pleasure filled the air around him just as Jakob realized he'd forgotten to put on a condom.

"Damnit."

Her eyes flew open. "What?"

"I forgot a condom."

"I'm on the pill, and I'm clean."

He shuddered. "I promise I'm clean."

"I want you like this inside of me."

Those words were uttered with such hunger Jakob felt his control slipping. He knew there was one way he wanted her, and he pulled out of her before he lost all sense.

"Jake!"

He ignored her irritated shout to turn her over onto her

stomach, pulling her up by her hips and entering her once again.

"Oh," she gasped, then she moaned his name. A man couldn't ask for more than that. Well, other than feeling her come on his dick.

He started to move, their flesh slapping, her moans...each time he thrust inside of her, her inner muscles clamped tighter and tighter. His fingers dug into her flesh as he increased his rhythm. He lost track of everything but the sound of her pleasure and the feel of her each time he drove inside.

"Baby, touch yourself. I can feel you need to come again."

Before he had finished his sentence, she was already pressing against her clit in a fevered motion. In the next instant, she came, her moan so loud he was surprised that it didn't shatter the glass. All those fabulous muscles rippled over his shaft.

"Fuck, yes, just like that." With one more hard thrust, he lost himself to the pleasure.

She heard the birds first thing in the morning, like every morning. Lani stretched, then winced. She was definitely not accustomed to being that acrobatic during sex, but making love with Jakob had definitely worn her out. She'd lost count of the times they made love.

In fact, he had woken her up a little bit before dawn with his head between her legs.

Speaking of which, she opened her eyes and found herself alone. She frowned until she saw the message scribbled on a piece of paper on the pillow next to her.

Love,

I had to make a few calls and figured I should let you rest. Can't be in the same bed with you and not want you. I'll be downstairs.

She held the note to her chest. For the first time in a long time, she felt hope. Hope that maybe, just maybe, she and Jake might have a fighting chance to be together.

But first things first. She needed a shower, and then she definitely needed to eat.

Jakob hung up the phone. He'd had a production meeting that he had asked to do by phone instead of by Zoom. He'd also texted with his brother to check on Jules. All was well. She had moved back to their house the day he returned to Oahu. With both Nic and their mother there, they promised to make sure she would rest.

There was a knock on the door before it opened. Emily smiled at him.

"Did you get your stuff done?"

He nodded.

"Good."

Aaron, or Mad Dog, stepped up behind her.

"Em, what are you doing?"

"Shut your trap, Aaron."

Her brother ignored her. "Aaron Daniels," he said, holding out one massive paw. The man was built like a giant. Jakob took it to shake. "Most people call me Mad Dog."

"They do not," his sister said.

"Shut up."

"Of course, I remember when you were fighting."

"Here we go," Emily said, disgust filling her voice. Both men ignored her.

"You work for Dillon now?"

He nodded. "Someone has to keep track of Sprout."

"Ignore him. I'm sure you're hungry. Aaron makes the most amazing pancakes. I texted Lani, and she said she was coming."

Emily stepped back to let Jakob step out of the room.

"Excited about the new show," Aaron said as he walked away.

"Thanks."

"She's going to be here any minute, so I want to tell you that if you hurt her, I will end you."

He blinked.

Emily shook her head. "So prissy. I mean it. That idiot brother of hers is being an ass, and I need to know you will step up for her. I've only spent a week with her, but I get the feeling she doesn't have a lot of people in her corner. You need to be one of those people, or you need to get bent."

"I would have been here the moment all this happened if I hadn't been with my sister."

"Yes, and that earns you points with me. Good brothers are hard to come by. So, make sure you understand I *can* make you disappear. Now, look lively. Here comes the woman you love."

He cut a look at her. She shrugged. "You have goo-goo eyes every time you look at her."

"Hey, Jakob."

He walked to her then, his steps sure and steady. He slipped his arm around her waist the moment he could and pulled her against him.

"You look better this morning," he said, cupping her chin.

"Well, that's always good to hear from a guy. You don't look like shit."

"No." He rolled his eyes, then set his forehead against hers. "I'm sorry. You just looked a little fragile when I got here yesterday. You still are the most beautiful woman I've ever seen."

"Jakob, I need you not to lie to me. If this will work, I need you to be honest with me."

That sounded promising.

"What do you think I'm lying about?"

"That I'm the most beautiful woman you have ever seen. You are always surrounded by beautiful women."

"From the first time, I saw you in that turquoise bikini."

"You were rude as hell to me."

"You were underaged. And you were Ben's little sister."

Her eyes narrowed. "Why would that matter?"

"Which one? The underage thing. Because I'm not a groomer. And second, I had promised not to touch you."

She stepped away from him. "What the hell?"

"I had a reputation. And truthfully, I wouldn't have had anything to do with you. You were underaged, and that was not me."

"And since then? Is it because of my brother?"

He shrugged. "And you seemed to hate me. So, I steered clear."

"I am annoyed."

"I'm sorry."

"No. I am annoyed with my brother. He dated a couple of my friends. Granted, it was after we hit eighteen, but I lost friends because he was such an ass. I'll have a talk with him about that crap."

She snorted.

"So, Emily isn't your assistant."

"Actually, she is. But she has a few extra abilities."

"Like I can disappear, people," Emily said from behind him. He jumped because he hadn't heard her approach.

"Stop telling people that, Em."

"Why? It's true."

Then Emily took two fingers and pointed at her eyes and then at him.

In the next instant, her expression cleared. "Breakfast is ready. Come on."

He glanced at Lani, and she smiled at him. It was the kind of smile that showed her dimples and had her dark gaze sparkling.

"Did she just threaten me?" he asked.

Lani nodded. "I made sure to tell Mad to make pancakes. I know you love them, and he has a fantastic recipe."

Jealousy hit him so hard that he almost growled in response. He wasn't a man who got jealous about his lovers. But the idea that Mad Dog had made her breakfast didn't sit well.

Her eyes widened. "Did you just growl?"

"No." Yes. "Maybe."

"Come on. Let's eat so we can tell you everything."

She took his hand, threading her fingers through his, and something in his chest moved. It was like his whole world settled whenever she touched him. Things seemed calmer.

They sat around the table, going over things once again.

"So, when I couldn't reach you, I ran."

"To Conner Dillon."

He spat out the other man's name. "What?"

"Nothing."

"Hollywood's jealous," Emily said in a stage whisper.

His expression turned even darker.

"He isn't. That would be stupid."

"Everything's stupid when feelings are involved," Emily said. She turned to look at Jakob. "There's no reason. That man is insanely in love with his wife. Other women don't exist on that level for him. He sees them as friends and coworkers. That's it. I need to clean up the dishes and give you a few moments alone with Hollywood."

Emily gathered the plates and headed out of the dining room. Lani rolled her eyes and looked at Jakob. "Sorry about that."

"She was right."

"What?"

He rose out of his chair and took her hand, pulling her up. Stepping closer, he cupped her face with both hands. "I was jealous. I *am* jealous. Thinking that you ran to any man other than me irritates me."

"There is no need."

"I'm sorry, Lani."

"For what?"

"I should have waited until you returned. I should have been there when you came in scared."

The last week had been horrible, not knowing who was after her and thinking that someone wanted her dead. Tears filled her eyes.

"Please don't cry. It kills me to see you like this."

"I hate being a coward."

"Who the fuck called you a coward?"

"No one. Me. I don't like running."

"You didn't run. You took time out to regroup. I take it they have a lead on the person?"

She shook her head. "Everyone we suspected has alibis for at least one of the incidents."

He used his thumbs to wipe away her tears, then bent his head to brush his mouth over hers. Just like every other time he kissed her, heat exploded within her, racing through her blood, making her want him. She would never understand how she could go from normal to a raging inferno, but it only happened with Jakob.

Slanting his mouth over hers, he deepened the kiss as he slipped his hands down her body, skimming his fingers against the side of her breasts before slipping them around her waist to her back. He pressed her against him, and there was no denying the long, thick length of him pressed against her. It had been a long two weeks, and she needed this, needed him in a way she had never needed another person.

Lani was close to suggesting they either lock the door to the dining room or head to her room when she heard Emily clearing her throat.

"Psst, guys, sorry, but I have to break this up."

With a growl, Jakob tore his mouth away from Lani.

"Go away."

Emily smiled. "Wow. That was sexy, but I can't. The big bossman is on his way up the drive and will want to talk to both of you."

Jakob sighed and looked at her. He settled his forehead against hers. "To be continued?"

"Definitely."

"Ah, you two are so cute."

"*Emily.*"

"Don't worry, love."

Somewhere in the distance, she heard the murmur of male voices. In the next instant, Conner appeared with Aaron.

"Good, you're both here. We have a problem."

Jakob stepped aside, but he slipped his arm around Lani's waist and anchored her against him. Whatever Conner had to say, they would deal with it together. Lani wanted to cry again because...well, having someone in her corner was amazing. She had Emily and the entire Dillon Security team, but having Jakob beside her was different.

She realized that Jakob and Conner knew each other in some way. Of course, they did. Dillon Security was the best security company on the islands, and being a Wulf meant they'd probably used them.

Then his words sunk in.

"What's wrong?"

"It seems your sister-in-law has disappeared."

FOURTEEN

They gathered in the living area of the house. Jakob made sure that Lani was right beside him. He had never thought of her as fragile, but he knew she was definitely feeling vulnerable at that moment.

"Royal's missing? How? I haven't heard from my brother."

"He's called a few times."

That came from Emily. She shrugged.

"You two needed to talk without the king boy bothering you."

There was something else there. Emily definitely did not like Ben. "You don't suspect him of going after Lani, do you?"

"I did."

"You're letting your personal feelings get in the way, Em," Lani said. That told Jakob there was more to the story than just this incident.

"Well, come on. Even Conner thought he might have had something to do with it."

"Everyone in her life was suspect."

Jakob looked at Conner, who studied him with a shrewd gaze. "I would never do anything to hurt Lani."

"I know, and I understand the feeling. But we had to check you out. Your relationship had been...different before now."

He drew in a deep breath. Jakob knew he could get mad about this or just let it go.

"Now, I was just with your brother, who has no idea where Royal is. He called us in."

"Maybe she got lost in her bedroom," Emily said. "It's not like a lot is going on up there."

"You would be wrong. I got some more information on her this morning as we started digging. Seems Royal has a border-line genius IQ."

"Good God, then why is she the way she is?" Emily asked.

"Emily," Conner said. His tone told Jakob that he was used to dealing with her antics.

"Sorry, but not really."

"And you still don't know who could be doing this?" Jakob asked. "Do you think it could be the same person?"

"We have two main suspects," Conner said. "Then a few competitors might have been trying to scare her away. There were a few family members at first, but they all checked out. In fact, none of them were overly happy with you being gone."

"Really? I always thought most of them would rather deal with my brother."

"No."

Conner was right. They had lost one big sponsorship for an invitational in Australia. Without Lani there to work on the contract, everything fell through.

"He took you for granted," Emily said.

"I have to agree with Emily," Jakob said. Lani looked at him, surprise lighting her eyes. "What? I've known that one reason Kingston remained successful over the years was your business sense."

"Yes, and that's why I tried to hire her away. I also plan to keep trying. It worked for a cover story, though. No one would wonder, at least for a couple of weeks, why she left for Miami, where our headquarters are located. So you haven't heard from Royal?" Conner asked.

She shook her head. "I haven't heard from her since that morning after the wedding."

"Okay. I have Ian working on it. He's at your brother's place with his new partner."

"What? Mix has a new partner?"

Conner stood. "He doesn't like that nickname, especially since everyone in Task Force Hawaii now calls him by it."

Emily giggled in delight. "Good, he's too stuffy." She turned to Lani. "He's excellent, though. Former MI-6 and all that. He's handled hostage negotiations before."

"And that might be what we have here, or it could be the same person after you. Either way, I want to bring your brother up to date."

"He's clear?" Emily asked, her voice telling him she didn't believe he wasn't. Granted, he was wondering about his best friend. This wasn't the man he had known for years. He could say one woman couldn't change you, but then...he looked at Lani. It had happened to him.

"Yes."

"Give me my phone, Em."

She handed it over to Lani. She texted someone—presumedly Ben. Then she stood. "I want to be there when we tell him."

Conner nodded. "That might be good. Your brother isn't handling this that well."

"My brother doesn't handle most bumps in the road well."

"I'm going to head over there again. I'll see you in a bit."

She nodded.

"We'll get her there safe, boss," Emily said.

As soon as the front door shut, Emily shook her head.

"You think Conner doesn't realize you don't trust him?"

Lani sighed. "I trust Conner."

Emily looked at him, then Lani. She settled her hands on her hips. "Lani."

"I didn't want to say I still don't trust my brother. I love him, even after everything. But...now his wife is missing? I'm getting worried that this is bigger than we originally thought."

"I think someone trying to kill you is a big deal," Jakob said.

Both women looked at him. Lani looked irritated. Emily looked like she approved.

"I get that, but I think it might be beyond the personal. I mean, this might have to do with Kingston."

"We looked at that," Emily said.

"I know, but we might need to do a deep dive into things and see if anything was done before we took over. Kingston has been around for decades."

Of course, she was right. Lani was one of the smartest women he had ever met.

"Let's not worry about that right now. Let's get over to your brother's house."

Ian Smith watched Ben pace back and forth in front of the window. He shared a look with his new partner, Eden Carlyle. They had known each other for years. When he had been MI-6, she had been CIA. Small-boned with light blue eyes and blonde hair, most people who didn't know her would think she was fragile. Most would discover that she was lethal too late to save themselves.

"Mr. Kingston, I think you need to calm down," Eden said. "We're doing everything we can to find your wife."

"You're just standing here."

Another shared look. This time, he saw his own agitation reflected back at him. They knew how to play the game with someone like Kingston.

"We're here in case there's a call. We have other operatives out searching."

He stopped in his tracks. "Can't you track her phone?"

Panic tinged the edges of his voice. That was definitely real. "No. She has it turned off. We'll find it as soon as she turns it back on."

It could have been damaged in an abduction, but Ian wasn't about to say that. Keeping the client calm was the most important thing. His boss had stopped by and seemed to calm Kingston a little, but it hadn't taken long for the irritation, and he was sure fear to come back.

Before Kingston could say anything, the front door opened.

"Hey, Mix, we're here."

He rolled his eyes. Emily was a pain in his ass.

"Mix?" Eden asked, one eyebrow rising. He knew that look.

"No. You do *not* start using it."

Emily stepped into the room. "Mix, baby, how've you been?"

"I will not answer to that name. And I saw you yesterday."

Emily ignored him and walked further into the room. She was followed by Lani and Jakob. Ian didn't often get star-struck, but he was a Brit and a fan. He had been irritated that his sister had met his favorite actor before he had. He'd had to fight the need to gush over him when he'd taken him to Lani's safehouse.

"Eden? This is wonderful," she said, coming forward to hug the other woman.

"That's Lani and Hollywood."

"Jake? What are you doing here?"

"I was at Lani's when you texted."

And that told Ian that Ben's best friend might not trust him. From how he held onto Lani, Ian would bet it had every-thing to do with the woman.

Ben studied them, his gaze ping-ponging back and forth. "What the hell?"

Lani walked forward, her steps sure and her gaze locked on her brother. He had been brought up to speed about her rela-tionship with Ben and how it had deteriorated after he'd met Royal. But...he saw the love there. He also knew there had been Dillon agents with her constantly, and all of her communica-tions were being monitored.

She wrapped her arms around Ben.

"It's going to be okay." Her voice was barely above a whisper.

Her brother hesitated, then wrapped his arms around her and held on tight.

"I'm worried something happened to her. Something bad."

Emily muttered something under her breath, but at least she kept it quiet enough that their clients didn't hear her.

"Dillon is good. They will do everything in their power to find her."

Ian noticed that Lani didn't say she would be alive, but then she was a lawyer.

She pulled away from her brother and looked at Ian. "Any news?"

He shook his head. "I called in a favor with TFH and their Team Bravo. That's their search and rescue group."

"I can pay for someone. We don't need to use state resources," Ian said.

"Mate, they're the best," Wulf said.

"And Ian has an in with them," Eden said. "His sister is married to the guy in charge of search and rescue."

"Plus, there are only a handful of search and rescue groups here," Ian said. As if on cue, the doorbell rang.

"Hot men with guns. Just my type," Emily said, turning to answer the door.

The murmur of voices filled the foyer, and then Emily led them back to the living space. Some of his worry settled as he watched his brother-in-law lead his team into the room.

"Hey, Ian, I heard you need help."

Jakob nodded to Team Bravo as they filled the room. He'd met the five-person team when he met with Adam Lee, the leader of Team Alpha. That's when it hit him with what Smith had said.

"You're Autumn's brother?"

He nodded. They didn't look that much alike except around the eyes.

Then he turned to study Team Bravo. The newly formed team's primary focus was search and rescue, while he knew they were building another team to take care of terrorism threats. This was a five-person team with the leader, Seth Harrington. He knew the other man had been a SEAL, as had Rami Ramirez, another team member. Standing to the right of Seth was Ryan Morrison, the dog handler. He'd heard he was from California, as was Maya, his dog. She sat patiently by his side.

A rather tall African American fellow stood directly behind Seth. Kap had been a member of NCIS and was staring daggers at Eden, but she was pretending to ignore him. Then, there was the lone woman on the team. Nikki Kekoa was a fierce Hawaiian who had been in the Coast Guard.

"We've been briefed by Dillon," Seth said. "We have Charity keeping an eye on her phone, and she will contact us as soon as she comes back online."

"But what do we do until then?" Ben asked. He sounded so much older than he had yesterday.

He glanced at his friend. Yeah, worrying about someone you love would do that to you.

"We need to go over her friends and her habits. We also need her recent clothing for Maya. I understand that her car is missing?"

That was news to him. He watched Ben nod. As if on cue, Seth's phone rang. He frowned when he looked down at the screen.

"Hello." Then he listened. "Sam—"

Whatever was being said had him quiet.

"We don't need her help," Ian muttered, but Seth ignored him as he listened.

"Gotcha. I take it I don't want to know how you found that out?"

There was a humming silence. "Thanks, Sam."

He hung up and glanced at Ian, then back to them. "We've found her car. It's at the entrance to Wailea Falls."

The site was popular with tourists and locals who liked to hike.

"Ben, did Royal like to go there?" Lani asked.

"Not sure. She hiked, but it was more...recreational, you know? Like, she didn't like to do too much when hiking."

"We're still going to need an article of clothing. That way, we can follow it from the car."

Ben nodded and left to get it. Lani walked over to Jakob. "What do you think?"

He shrugged. "I don't know her well. Maybe they had an argument, and she went off. He mentioned that when Royal didn't get her way, she tended to go off alone."

Lani nodded, worry stamping her face. He wrapped his arms around her.

"Everything will work out," he said, kissing her temple.

"What the fuck?" Ben said as he stepped into the living room.

Lani looked back at her brother. "I think you have other things to worry about, Ben."

His eyes narrowed, but he handed a robe to Seth. "She wore this last night."

"That should work."

"I'm going with you."

"No, sir, you need to stay here," Seth said. "What if she heads back before we get there? Or, if she was kidnapped, you will need to talk to them to negotiate. I think you should be here to wait for news."

He could see the irritation on Ben's face, but his friend nodded. "Thanks for your help."

"Of course, sir. Your sister expects a call, Mix."

"That is not my name."

A few of the people on the team chuckled as they walked out.

"Should I go with them?" Emily asked. She had been subdued, which Jakob assumed wasn't normal for her. That told him that everyone was worried about Royal.

"No. Stay here because we need to monitor their search and a few other things we are checking on," Ian said.

"Who was that who called?"

"No one."

"Sam," Eden said at the same time.

"I am going to need to know more after we are done with this emergency," Emily said to her coworkers.

Seth Harrington had an awful feeling as he and his team approached the car. It was still early, but there were people around. One thing they would have was people to question. If this is just a wealthy wife being pissed off with her husband, it might turn out easy.

His gut told him it wouldn't be that easy.

"Well, shit," Kap said, looking inside the car. "We have blood. A lot of blood."

Seth stepped closer to look and realized Kap hadn't been

exaggerating. There was a good chance that if they found Royal Jones-Kingston, it would be a recovery.

Maya barked and headed off in the direction of the walking path. They all fanned out and started the search. He knew if there was a chance of Royal being alive, they didn't have long.

The tension in the house was almost unbearable, but Lani couldn't force herself to leave her brother. It wasn't a good sign when a newly married woman went missing.

"So, you're working for Dillon."

His tone was so damned condescending she wanted to smack him. She loved Ben, but he was pushing his luck. Yes, she knew this was his way of avoiding the situation. Either Royal left him, or she was taken. Either scenario was bad. Still, she wasn't going to put up with his BS.

"Yes."

"And you're fucking my best friend."

"Watch that tone," Jakob said, his voice a lethal rumble. She shouldn't find it so sexy, but it was. It was the same growl he used when they were alone.

"I warned you to keep your hands off her."

"I think you need to..." his words finally registered. Lani looked between the two men. "Wait, what?"

It took a full ten seconds for Ben to break his angry eye contact with Jakob.

"When I met him, I told him he couldn't touch you."

Her eyes widened, then they narrowed.

"That was years ago. What does that have to do with what's going on now?"

"You're my little sister. There's a code."

She rolled her eyes. Yes, she knew they had an audience, but she didn't care.

"A code? The same code you had with Rick?"

"No. That's different."

"How? Because you two have always been pretty chummy, and you didn't have a problem with me fucking him?"

"It's different."

"No. It's not."

Jakob stepped up beside her. She glanced at him. While she appreciated his silent support, she wasn't that happy with him.

"I'll deal with you later."

"Is there any popcorn in this house," Emily said, cutting through some of the tension.

"I have no idea. Probably," Lani said.

"You quit, then you take up with him," her brother said, his voice full of self-righteousness.

"I didn't quit. You fired me. And, I will take up with whomever I want. Jake is who I want."

"I don't like your choice."

"Are you freaking kidding me, bra? The woman you married hated the sight of me. I figured she's the one who talked you out of having breakfast last Sunday."

"Breakfast? What are you talking about? And what do you mean I fired you?"

"Royal said we would have breakfast before you left for your honeymoon. Later that day, I was fired via text."

"I did not fire you. Also, we weren't leaving right away."

She blinked. "What? You were supposed to leave Sunday night."

He shook his head. "We planned to go later because of Royal's condition."

A sinking feeling filled her. She knew the answer before she asked it.

"What condition?"

"Royal was pregnant."

All of a sudden, everything started to make sense. Ben had never been that serious about settling down before meeting Royal and even after meeting her. Then, all of a sudden, they were planning a wedding, and he was enthusiastic about it. She had just chocked it up to falling in love, which was probably part of it. The other part of it had been an unplanned pregnancy.

Awkward silence still filled the room when Emily broke it. "We seriously need some popcorn for this."

"Em," Ian warned. Then he turned his attention to her brother. "Was? Why are you talking about your wife in the past tense?"

Ben shoved a hand through his hair. "She lost the baby three days after the wedding."

Her heart ached. She might not like Royal, but Ben loved her, and she knew that Ben would have loved that baby.

"Ben," she said, walking toward her brother and slipping her arms around him. She wasn't sure what kind of reception she would get from him. When his arms wrapped around her, she held on tight. They had always had each other, and while she wasn't that happy with Royal, Lani loved her brother. And she would have loved any baby he had with Royal.

"I'm sorry," she whispered.

"I was too."

Ian's phone went off. He looked down at the screen. "I have to take this."

He left them in the room as Lani stepped back from hugging her brother. His soft gaze hardened as he looked at Jakob.

"I think you and I need to talk," Ben said.

"I think not," she said. At the same time, Jakob said, "Fine with me."

As Jakob walked closer, Lani stepped in front of him. She settled her hand on his chest. Her brother's growl irritated. "I don't need you defending my honor."

He lifted his hand and cupped her face. Ben growled again, but Jakob also ignored him.

"Love, I would defend it until the day I die." He brushed his mouth over hers, then looked at her brother. "Let's go to your study."

His brother strode off. Jakob followed easily as if he didn't have a care in the world.

Ian stepped back into the room. "Where's Ben?"

"He's going all big brother on Jakob," Emily said. "Any news."

"Yeah, and none of it is good. They found blood on her car."

Lani sighed. None of this felt like it would end with a happily ever after.

FIFTEEN

J akob kept his arms loose at his sides as he followed his best friend into his study. It didn't seem like the right time to have this conversation. Still, he figured it would be a good way to distract Ben. Ben was staring out the window, looking at the ocean and the horizon.

"You want to tell me what the fuck is going on with my sister?"

There was a tone in his voice that Jakob couldn't decipher. Ben definitely sounded angry, but there was something else... something that almost sounded like he was hurt. He knew this was important. Even after all their issues, Ben and Lani were close. He didn't want to be the thing that tore them apart.

Not wanting anyone else to hear the conversation, he shut the door and walked further into the room.

"Are you not going to answer me?"

"I would rather look at you when I answer...not the back of your head."

There was a long, strained beat of silence before he started to turn around. Once Ben met his gaze...there was no denying the anger burning within the dark depths of his gaze. It should scorch him. He didn't have a lot of true friends in the world. His money and fame made it hard to determine who he could trust. Jakob knew, without a doubt, that he could trust Ben. So he couldn't and wouldn't lie.

"I'm in love with her."

"Give me a break."

Jakob rolled his eyes. "I'm telling you the truth. I've been in love with her for years."

Before his friend could respond, there was a knock at the door.

"Come in," Ben said.

Ian was at the door. "I have news. They found her car, and they are now searching for her."

"That's it?"

"Yes. I'll let you get back to that," he said, motioning with his hand.

Once they were alone again, Ben studied him. "I don't have time for this right now."

"Time for what?"

"Beating the shit out of you."

He snorted. "Have fun trying, mate. But know this, at the end of the day, I will still love her, and there's nothing you can do about it.

Seth followed Ryan and Maya as they led the way on the trail. It was already starting to get hot, and there were no trades giving them any relief. Maya was hot on the trail, and the heaviness in Seth's gut told him this wouldn't have a happy ending.

"Bad vibes," Rami said next to him as they jogged along, both of them keeping their eyes moving to keep site of any other clues as to her whereabouts. Rami was a former SEAL like him, and both had learned to trust their gut. Training was essential, but instincts were just as important.

Seth nodded as they continued on their way, and when he heard Maya's excited barks, he knew it wasn't a good sign.

"There's a Rick here to see Ben," Eden said, walking into the room. She had gone to chat on the phone, so it apparently was to deal with that.

"Send that loser packing," Emily said.

"No. He'll just come back. He has never learned to understand that he wasn't wanted. And, he might have something to talk to Ben about."

Emily didn't look happy about it, but Eden did her bidding.

Rick came into the living area and started to make a beeline for Ben's study when he noticed Lani. He changed directions.

"Lani, when did you get back?"

There was a tone in his voice, something that felt off.

"I've been on the island."

"That wasn't our cover story," Emily said, ignoring the other woman.

"My brother's talking to Jake right now. Is there something I can help you with?"

"You don't work for the company anymore," Emily said.

"I'm still a board member. If it has something to do with Kingston, I can at least see if I can help. My brother has too much on his plate right now."

He glanced at the other two women, then back to Lani. "Can we do this privately?"

Emily opened her mouth. "You've already checked him out. You know he isn't at fault here. We'll just step out on the lanai. You will be able to see us there."

Emily didn't look happy about it, but she nodded. "I'll keep watch on you the entire time." She was looking at Rick when she said that. He nodded and tried to take Lani's hand. She drew away from him and walked to the sliding door that led to the lanai.

"What's up, Rick?"

He sighed. "I broke up with Sienna."

And that was supposed to be important to her for what reason? Now that she had had months away from the insanity of her relationship with Rick, she knew how ill-suited they were for each other. He was still a cheater and probably always would be. She had known that going in, so part of it was on her.

"Okay. What does that have to do with Kingston?"

"It doesn't. Not really. I mean…" He glanced behind her into the living space, then stepped further away. He headed over to a shaded area and motioned her over. "I don't want to embarrass myself in front of strangers."

She shook her head and followed. The guy was stupid as the day was long, even if he was an excellent surfer. It would be best to put this to rest once and for all.

When she stepped into the shade, she felt a bit of relief. The morning sun was heating up the day, and the trades were non-existent.

"So?"

"I'm sorry."

"Nice to know. What are you sorry about? The cheating? Or was it the number of times you fucked someone else? Or the fact that you fucked Sienna in my bed?"

He blinked. "I'm sorry for it all. I was stupid, but you don't understand. There was something else going on. Something that Royal knew all about."

There was another knock at Ben's study door, and this time, Ian came right in after the knock.

"They found your wife, Mr. Kingston."

Hope flared to life in Ben's eyes. "And?"

"I'm sorry."

And then, Jakob watched the color drain from his best friend's face. Ian rushed in and grabbed him just as Jakob reached out for him. He had been worried that Ben would pass out.

"Was she in an accident?"

"No. She was murdered."

"Where's Lani?" Jakob asked.

"She's in the living area with Eden and Emily."

He turned, but Ben stopped him. "What's going on, Jakob. I saw the look on your face."

"Your sister has been threatened several times, and we think it might all be tied together."

Jakob couldn't put a finger on his emotion or explain why

he was feeling it. Something unsettled him enough to have him rushing down the hall.

"What did she know about?"

This was the most bizarre conversation. He kept pacing back and forth and wringing his hands.

"There was nothing I could do."

"Okay."

Suddenly, he surged toward her, and now, the alarm screamed through her system. She tried to step back, but he grabbed her by her upper arms. "I need to protect you. I don't know who did it, but someone did, and they will probably come after you."

Panic had her opening her mouth to scream. She was amazed that Eden and Emily hadn't come rushing out. When he yanked her forward, she tried to glance behind her. From this position, the ladies couldn't see them.

"Rick, you need to let me go."

"She wanted me to. She wanted me to do that the entire time. But I couldn't do it. I didn't want to let you go." He was now babbling as he dragged her away from the house. His fingers were digging into her skin. She was sure there would be bruises. Even in the day's heat, she was freezing, her body shivering from the bone-chilling fear seeping into her soul.

"Rick."

He looked at her, his eyes widening at something behind her.

"Get your bloody hands off her," Jakob roared from behind her.

"I'm trying to save her, man. You don't understand." But he did let her go.

Jakob grabbed her and spun her around.

"Love, are you okay?"

She blinked at him, her head still spinning from the turn of events. The fury in his gaze sent alarm racing through her.

"He didn't hurt me," she said. "Everything is fine."

"The hell it is," he said, handing her off to someone behind him. She realized it was Emily.

"Sorry, Lani. I turned away when Jakob came running down the hall."

"It was a split second. Not your fault."

"Argh!"

She whipped her head around to see Jakob had tackled Rick. They were rolling over the grass, punching each other. Correction, Rick was trying his damndest to get away, and Jakob was beating the living hell out of him. He ended up on top of Rick and started to pummel the other man.

"Mate, you're going to kill him," Ian said, although he didn't do anything to stop Jakob.

Lani stepped closer. "Jake, please stop."

He didn't seem to hear her. The scene before her was wavering, and she realized she was crying. She wasn't worried about Rick but didn't want anything to happen to Jake.

"Please let him go. I need you," she said, hoping that would get his attention. And apparently, that was all she needed to say. He stopped in mid-punch and turned around. Rising to his feet, he approached her and took Lani into his arms.

"Don't cry, love. I didn't hurt him that much."

"I don't care about that idiot. I'm worried about the man I love going to jail for assault."

There was a long beat of silence that seemed to stretch and stretch.

He pulled back and looked down at her, cupping her face. Using his thumbs, he brushed away her tears. "I love you, too."

He dipped his head and brushed his mouth over hers as her heart filled with joy. Even in this horrible moment, she could find happiness.

Lani turned and saw that Ian was on the phone, probably with an ambulance service, because Rick was unconscious.

An hour later, things were still in an uproar. HPD, TFH, and every other letter agency known to man were at the house. Lani was resting far away from the trouble in the guest house as Jakob watched HPD and TFH argue about who had jurisdiction.

"Don't worry, Hollywood. We won't let them throw you in the slammer."

He shook his head. "Not really worried about that."

Emily sighed. "Sorry about what happened."

Surprised, he looked at the woman. She shrugged. "It was my job to protect your lady."

"And I distracted you. Don't worry about it."

Conner Dillon came striding into the house, taking in the scene and nodding in their direction. "You might not worry, but that man is going to eat my lunch."

He made his way over to them. "I need to see you both in another room."

Emily and Jakob shared a look.

"Wait. What are you doing?" That came from HPD detective Rome Carino.

"Talking to my client. We will not discuss the assault. It's about my client's safety."

"We won't leave the house," Jakob promised.

They went into the kitchen.

"What's up, boss?"

"We have an issue. There is no way that Rick carried out all of the attacks."

"Lani said it sounded like he had been working with Royal."

"Yes. We are still digging, but apparently, those two used to work a lot of cons together. Some blackmail. That's not what has me worried. We are missing something. Royal and Rick were both cleared for the parking garage incident. They either hired someone else, or we are missing something."

Lani stepped out of the bedroom and started when she saw who was standing in the living room of the guest house.

"Sienna, what are you doing here?"

"I've been looking for you."

The woman was a mess. Her hair looked like she hadn't brushed it. There was dirt on her face. As Lani walked closer, she realized her shirt was soaked with blood.

"Sienna, are you okay? Did someone hurt you?"

"Yes," she said, raising a gun and pointing at Lani. "You did."

Sixteen

Jakob, Dillon, and Emily were halfway across the yard when they heard the gunshot. For the second time in less than two hours, his heart stopped. Even as he started running through the yard, he heard the shouting inside the main house. He ignored it. He knew that the gunshot had come from the guest house, and Lani was the only person in there. Or she had been until some bastard got through all the police protection around the area.

Ignoring Dillon's shout, he busted the door open. His attention was pulled to Lani, who lay on the floor, then to the woman standing over her.

Sienna looked to be readying for another shot at Lani when she swung her arm toward him. Dillon grabbed him and yanked him out of the way. Then, he heard the shot of a gun, but it was much closer than he thought. That's when he noticed that Emily had a gun out and had shot into the house. Ian was there backing her up, as was HPD Detective Carino.

He fought against Dillon's hold. "Wait until they give the all-clear. It's the only way you can make sure Lani's safe."

"She was shot."

"She was down. You don't know if she was shot."

"Clear!" Emily yelled out.

That was all he had to hear. Jakob rushed back in, panic filling him as he ran to Lani. She was so still on the floor. Ian was checking her pulse.

"Strong pulse. I think she hit her head on the way down."

Jakob pushed him out of the way and patted Lani down. Where was she shot?

"Man, I don't think she was shot."

"Then why is she out cold? She has to be shot." What the hell would he do without her? They were finally together. He couldn't lose her.

"Coming through," someone called out.

"Man, the EMTs are here. They'll find out what's wrong with her."

He didn't want to let her go. She was so still, and he knew she would drift away if he didn't keep touching her. Jakob knew it didn't make much sense.

"Jake, come on. Let them look at my sister."

He glanced up and noticed that Ben was standing close by. His friend seemed to have aged five years in the last two hours. Using all of his control, he did as Ben had asked.

The EMT and his partner did a quick check. "She was grazed on the shoulder, but..." he felt her head and nodded. "I think she also hit her head. That's why she's unconscious."

"I'm not unconscious. Not anymore."

Her irritated voice was the sweetest sound Jakob had ever heard.

"Love," he said, moving closer. The female attendant took a look at Jakob and nodded. "I'm going to deal with the shooter."

She moved away, and he took her place. Lani was still too still. She kept her eyes closed so Jakob took hold of her hand.

"Ms. Kingston, can you open your eyes?"

"I could. I have a feeling the light will hurt."

"I need to check for a possible concussion."

She sighed.

"Love, do it for me," he said.

With what seemed to be a great deal of effort, Lani opened her eyes. The EMT used a small light. "We'll need to take you to the hospital to have you checked out. It looks like you could have a concussion, and you will need to have a doctor look at your shoulder."

Her fingers spasmed around his hand. "I'll go with you, Lani. Don't worry."

Her sigh of relief was quiet but reassuring. "Good."

Then she closed her eyes. "Tell me when I have to open my eyes again."

"I think I should be able to go home," Lani said, ready to scream. It was just after seven that night, and she wanted to sleep in her bed. Or Jakob's. Just not the hospital bed.

"You need to stay in the hospital."

"I feel fine. Therefore, I need to go home."

He looked up from a script he was looking over. He'd had Marta bring it over so he could spend all his time acting like some kind of warden to her.

"Are you telling me you received your medical degree on top of being a lawyer?"

She narrowed her eyes. "No."

"Oh, good. I was worried you were way out of my league. Now you're just a little out of it. No worries. I'll make up for it."

Then he went back to reading his script. The door swung open to reveal Emily.

"Em, good. Can you get me sprung from here?"

She looked from Lani to Jakob, who shook his head. Her gaze moved back to Lani. "Sorry. You aren't my job anymore."

"You're my friend. I need out of here."

"You have a concussion. You were shot."

"It was a graze."

Jakob opened his mouth to say something, but Emily stepped in.

"There was a rather hot older version of you at the nurses' station when I came in. Is that your brother?"

"Jensen's here?"

She nodded. "Go. I'll make sure she doesn't make a break for it."

He hesitated for a moment, then stood. After setting the script down on the bedside table, he turned back to her.

"Try your best to rest, please."

He kissed her forehead and headed out.

The moment the door shut, she opened her mouth, but Emily stopped her.

"Nope. I will not help you. Even if I was still your protection, I wouldn't. Not after how I saw Jakob react."

"What do you mean?"

Emily walked over to the window and settled in a chair. "He acted as if his entire world had fallen apart."

Lani looked away from her. "I was fine."

"He didn't know that. When someone is in love with you, it doesn't matter if you are fine. Those few minutes that the worst fear is realized...that shows who you truly are. For Jakob, he was ready to burn the entire damned world down. You're lucky."

Lani looked back at her friend. It had only been a week since they'd reconnected at the Dillon offices, but she knew she and Emily would be forever friends.

"Have you heard anything about what happened with Royal, Rick, and Sienna?"

She rolled her eyes. "Mix has been texting me info he's getting from his sister. I'm not sure he's supposed to do that."

The door opened, and Jakob came in, followed by his brother Jensen. Older by a few years, Jensen had always been the bad boy. There was always a dangerous air about him. There was no mistaking that the two men were brothers, but their personalities were completely different. Jensen could be a bit on the stuffy side.

"Lani, I'm sorry for what you went through," he said, kissing her cheek. She heard a noise that came from Jakob's direction.

Jensen shook his head. "Ignore him. He's a little out of sorts."

"Move aside," Jakob said, then he took up his spot once again.

"Em, this is Jensen, Jakob's older brother."

Jensen nodded in her direction.

"She was just going to tell us what was going on."

"Yes, Rick and Royal have been blackmailing people for the last four years. High society women who want a walk on the dangerous side. Or, I guess, older men who wanted to have affairs."

"It makes no sense what they were doing with me. Why would they come after me?"

"That is still a little hazy. Apparently, Royal actually did think she was pregnant, so she thought it would be best to kick you to the curb. If you weren't around, there would be more emphasis on the child getting all the money."

Lani shook her head. "Everyone keeps saying she was smart, but she didn't read the will too closely. She wouldn't have had access to the money. There would be three Kingston family guardians, just like we had when Mom and Dad died."

"She might have thought your brother would change the will." She shrugged. "Who knows? According to Rick, you were just supposed to get scared. Also, he claims he loves you and will earn your forgiveness."

"What the fuck?" Jakob said.

Emily chuckled. "Yeah, that apparently gave that Carino guy a good chuckle."

"Was he the one who tried to run me down?"

"Oh, no. That was Sienna. She is one crazy woman. She has been obsessed with Rick for years, and when Royal introduced them, she thought it was a dream come true. Unfortunately, he was still hung up on you. Seems this entire con didn't go that well."

"It sounds like a rubbish plan," Jensen said.

"You sound much more British than Hollywood over there."

Jensen smirked at Jakob.

"But you are right. If what Lani says is true, it doesn't make any sense. I'm sure it's like I said. She just thought she could convince your brother to disown you."

"Sienna is fine, by the way. My aim was true. Just hit her

shoulder. She's being held under guard. Also, she might be able to get off using insanity because, from what I hear, she is completely nuts. They think she might have killed Royal."

"Why would she do all this?"

"She was in love with Rick. She saw both of you as standing in her way." Emily shook her head. "I heard her yelling as they loaded her up in the ambulance. Anyway, I have to debrief the boss, who is waiting to chew me out."

"What the hell?" Lani said. "You did nothing wrong."

"I let Rick get hold of you."

She rolled her eyes. "He wasn't going to hurt me."

"Still, we didn't know that at the time. Hollywood, make sure you keep me up to date when she gets out. I dropped all your stuff off with Marta like you asked."

"I...I thought we could go back to my apartment."

"First, that's a bad idea. Reporters have found out, so they are hanging out at your place. Also...apparently, Sienna broke in and wrecked the place. She was caught on the security cameras we had installed."

Lani sighed, suddenly feeling more tired than five minutes ago.

"We'll get it cleaned up, love. Don't worry about it."

"Yeah, she mainly trashed electronics. Seriously, I should have seen how crazy she was. She had those kinds of eyes. Remember to text me."

Then she was gone.

"How's Jules?" Lani asked Jensen.

"Loud and very...just loud. She does not like being stuck in bed. I just wanted to pop over here and check on you two. I'm staying at the house tonight, but I will probably head back to Maui tomorrow after you leave."

After talking a bit longer about Jules and her situation, Lani felt her eyes drooping.

"You need your rest," Jensen said. "They will come in here and wake you up every few hours, so get your rest while you can."

"Thanks for coming, Jensen."

He smiled at her. "I had to. Can't let my baby brother handle all this on his own. I know how it feels to have your heart ripped out."

Jensen's now wife had been stalked at one point.

"Thanks, brother," Jakob said.

With that, he left them alone.

"I'm going to turn down the lights."

"You don't have to stay."

"Yes, I do."

She thought back to what Emily had said.

"Jake?"

"Yes, love?"

"Did we really profess our love to each other before everyone?"

His mouth twitched as he returned to the bed after shutting off the overhead lights. "Yes, we did. I'm sure he will yell at me once your brother deals with everything."

Her brother had stopped by, but he had been forced to leave her to go identify Royal's body.

"Who cares?"

"You do. You love Ben."

"Yes, but I choose you."

He moved to sit in the chair, but she shook her head. She scooted over, thankful she was no longer nauseous. He joined her on the bed.

"If you were wondering, I will always choose you, Lani. Any day of the week, any condition."

Tears filled her eyes as she snuggled closer. Even after everything that had happened in the last week—hell, even considering what happened today—she was happy. They weren't perfect, and she didn't know exactly where they would go from this point, but they had each other.

In the quiet of her hospital bed, she drifted off with Jakob's arms wrapped tight around her.

Epilogue

Three weeks later

"So, what do you think?" Jakob asked as they stood on the lanai of his new home.

He'd decided to pick an area closer to Honolulu since he would be filming there. Also, he thought, he couldn't get over the view. He'd found the house by chance in the Manoa Wood-lawn area of Honolulu. It was a bit cooler in the hills and boasted a ton of acreage—not that common for the region. It was also off the beaten path. Not a lot of celebrities lived in this particular area.

There had been a lot of changes over the last three weeks. The hospital had released Lani the day after the shooting. He had done everything he could to force her to rest, but she had been crafty. She'd convinced him she needed him near her to rest. She ended up seducing him—not that it was that hard to do.

Rick had pleaded guilty. He had made noises about fighting it, but it was easy enough to recover Royal's second phone. She hadn't erased any of their conversations. Messages were going back at least four years on that phone. California and Australia were also investigating, and Jakob was sure various other charges would come soon.

Sienna was currently being observed, tested, and interviewed. According to the DA, she would probably be found noncompetent. Rick had not been the first celebrity she had obsessed over, but he had been the only one she'd ended up dating. Her long history of mental breaks would probably give credence to the not guilty due to the insanity verdict. He heard that she was still asking for Rick.

"I like it," Lani said. "A lot. I told you that when we looked at it the first time."

And now came the uncomfortable part. His palms were sweaty, his head and heart were pounding, and his throat was closing up.

"Could you see yourself living here?"

She glanced over at him, holding onto her hair. The trades were insane today, but he liked it when they whipped her hair about.

"Are you asking me to move in with you?"

He shook his head, and she frowned.

"Oh."

He didn't understand the tone.

"I don't want us to just *live* together."

Her brow furrowed as she studied him in silence.

He sighed. "I am cocking this up, aren't I?"

"I don't know what this is."

He stepped closer and took her free hand.

"I want you to live here with me as my wife." Her eyes widened, but she still said nothing. Jakob plowed ahead. "I know it's fast. It's insanely fast, but when you know, you know. And I know. I know I want to marry you and have babies with you. I want to hang out together watching TV. I want to be with you always. And I understand if you want to wait. And I also understand if you want a long time to plan a big wedding. I'll wait. As long as you want me to."

She blinked a few times. "I don't want a big wedding. Something small with mainly family and very close friends."

His heart turned over. "Are you saying yes?"

Her expression was serious, then...her lips curved. "Jakob Wulf, I love you. Of course, I'll marry you."

There was a beat of silence before what she'd said registered.

"Yes!" Then he grabbed her up off the ground and spun her around.

She was giggling. "Put me down before you make me sick. You know I get motion sickness."

He set her down, then pulled a velvet box out of his pocket. "I had this made, but if you don't like it, we can get something else."

Popping the box open, he showed her the ring. A square diamond sat within a platinum setting made up of plumeria flowers. Twisting vines encircled the piece, and a rose gold thread was in the inlay pattern. He heard the click of her swallow.

"Jake, it's stunning." When she looked up at him, her eyes were filled with tears.

Happiness warmed him as he took the ring out and slipped it on her finger. It fit perfectly.

"I love it."

He pulled her into his arms. "I love you."

Bending down, he brushed his mouth over hers and was

thinking about taking it much further to celebrate, until he heard someone clearing their throat. With regret, he pulled back and looked over his shoulder. Ben stood at the gate that led to the backyard.

The last few weeks had been hard on Ben. Not that Jakob didn't think his best friend kind of deserved some of it, but he hated seeing his friend suffer. Ben and Lani had talked once or twice, but Jakob knew they needed to clear the air.

"I guess she took pity on you, huh?" Ben asked. He was dressed down, even for him. His Kingston Surfing t-shirt, which had seen better days, was tucked into a pair of khaki shorts.

"Wait, Ben knew?" Lani asked.

Jakob nodded, looking down at her. Her eyes were narrowed on him. "What?"

"Please tell me you didn't do something stupid and ask his permission. That will just piss me off."

He snorted. "No. I asked for his help with the ring. I created the design, but I wanted a second opinion."

Her expression cleared. "I love my ring."

Jakob smiled. "I have a phone call to make, so I thought you two could talk."

Leaning down to kiss her cheek, he whispered, "Try and clear the air, love. You both need to move on."

She nodded, but he could tell she had gone on her guard. Jakob understood. The man she had admired had been an ass the last year or so, and she wasn't ready to trust him just yet.

Walking to the house, he nodded to Ben and left them alone. He knew that Lani needed her brother, but Ben needed her more. Even with their insanely huge family, he was alone in the world now.

Lani didn't know what to say to her brother. He looked a mess, his hair needing a trim, and he had lost weight. They had spoken a few times since the insane events at the house, but it had been mainly over the phone.

"You look happy," Ben said, walking closer.

"I am."

He offered her a solemn smile. "Good. I never saw how much you two liked each other."

"I didn't like him. He was annoying."

His expression lightened. "I'm not sure if he wanted me to help him convince you to marry him or if he really wanted us to talk."

She rolled her eyes. "It didn't take much to convince me."

"Then, I guess it was mainly to let me talk to you. You look good."

"Thanks."

He sighed. "I don't know where I lost my way."

Lani stared at him. He was still the brother she loved, but so much had happened that she didn't know if she could trust him again. Not yet, at least. Lani waited. Usually, she would step in to make it easier for her brother, but Ben needed to fix things. At least, he needed to prove to her that he really wanted to fix this.

"I never believed in that hype around our name, you know." He shoved a hand through his hair. "Then, one day, I realized that it had been resting on my shoulders, and I didn't fuck it up. I started believing the hype. It wasn't me."

Now, she would step in. "Ben, you are good as the head of the company."

"I get that. Dad taught me just like Grandpa Ben taught him."

Just hearing the name invoked memories of his big laugh and even bigger hugs. "I miss him. Them."

He looked at her. "I miss my sister more."

For the second time that day, tears filled her eyes. "I miss you too, Ben."

"I'm not sure how we fix this."

She went to him then and took his hand. "We start by talking like this."

"Come back to Kingston, please."

She wanted that but on one condition. "I don't want to do PR. I want to use my law license."

Hope brightened his eyes. There. That was the look she remembered from her brother, before all the BS of the last year.

"You got it."

"And I want to work on contracts for Dillon Security."

He nodded and pulled her into one of his big hugs. "I'll try my best not to be a dick."

Another fresh wave of tears streamed down her face. She knew they had a lot to work on. She needed to speak up more and stand up for what she wanted. He needed not to be a dick.

"I've missed you." She leaned back and looked up at him. "I'm sorry about the baby."

"I am, too. Not sure if Royal and I would have made it, but I wanted that baby."

She squeezed him. "You would have been a great dad. And you will be when you find the right woman."

He rolled his eyes. "I am off the market for a while. I have a lot of work to do on myself and the company."

She nodded. "As long as you leave a day free to walk me down the aisle."

"Aw, Lani, you're gonna make me cry. I don't deserve it, but thank you. It would be my honor to walk you down the aisle."

"All better out here?" Jakob called out.

"He was really nervous about buying you that ring," Ben whispered loud enough for her to hear. That warmed her heart even more.

When she looked around her brother at Jakob, he frowned and strode over.

"Why are you crying?" He tugged her away from her brother and into his arms. "I said you could come over as long as you were nice to her."

She peeked at her brother, who looked amused at Jakob's antics.

"Jake, they're happy tears." She leaned back. "We're going to work on communicating more."

He sighed. "Good."

"How was your phone call?"

"It was fine."

"There was no phone call."

He shared a look with her brother. "Your sister already had my number. And no, there wasn't. But I did call in an order for lunch. It will be here soon. Come look at our new home, Ben. It has an elevator, which, according to Emily, makes me Ritchie Rich. She spent all her time in it during the walk-through."

Several Months Later

A light breeze filled the press area for the premiere on the beach for Task Force Honolulu. Jakob could hear the buzz of the fans that were filing in. The sun was sinking lower and lower, and his stomach was doing all sorts of somersaults.

As always, he looked for his constant. The one person who centered him. Lani was at the back of the press room, her smile shining. She had been the one who told him it was a good idea to have a premier on the beach. It was the day before the TV premiere, so the people of Hawai'i had a chance to see it first, as they should. It didn't take much for the studio to agree to it.

"How excited are you about the new premiere of Task Force Honolulu?" Simon Andrews asked Jakob, pulling him back into the conversation.

It was a stupid question, but he had played this game for a long time. "I'm beyond thrilled. I'm so glad the people of Hawai'i have accepted us."

He saw Emily roll her eyes. She stood next to Lani, ensuring no one bothered his fiancée. She wasn't on the job. She just saw it as her job to keep people from messing with Lani. Aaron was on the other side of Emily, his gaze always on alert. Ben stood next to Lani. The siblings had been working hard to repair their relationship, even if Ben took it to the extreme to become more of a workaholic.

There were a few more questions for him and the rest of the cast before it finally ended, and they could join the fans on the beach. He strode through the reporters to get to Lani.

The plans for their wedding were in full swing, but they were waiting until after he'd wrapped filming for the first season.

"Where do they get these idiot reporters?" Emily asked. "Like, if you didn't care about the show, you would have said so. Hey, Mix, what are you doing here?"

Sure enough, Ian, his sister Autumn, her husband, and the TFH Team Bravo were there. He had it on good authority that the agent still did not like his nickname.

"We got special tickets from Jake. Why are you here?"

"I'm Lani's bestie."

"Exactly," Lani said, fist-bumping Emily. His own family were making their way over to them. They were a little late, thanks to a major accident on the Pali Highway.

Seeing everyone there to support him almost had him tearing up. He had to be the luckiest man alive at the moment. "Let's all head down to the beach. The cast and our guests have an area set aside to sit.

He waited for everyone to file past, then slipped his arm around Lani's waist.

"Ready for your big premiere?" she asked, smiling up at him.

All his nerves dissolved. "I'm ready for anything with you by my side."

Together, they walked out of the press area and out into the rest of their lives.

A Note from Mel

Mahalo for reading the last book in The Wulf Series. I started writing this series 2017 before I was diagnosed with cancer. Thanks to that and the loss of my mother a month after I started chemo, things got pushed back, and it took me longer to finish off the series.

Task Force Hawaii is another series that is set in the Harmless World. There are actually two of them at the time of publishing this book: Task Force Hawaii and TFH Team Bravo. The original series is complete and available on all platforms. Justified Secrets (featuring Captain Seth Harrison and Autumn Bradford) is also available in wide distribution. There is a peek of their story!

Conner Dillon is the hero featured in Rough Fascination, and I am sure you will be happy to know that Dillon Security will have their own series in 2026.

ACKNOWLEDGMENTS

As always, no book is written without help. Thanks to Scott Carpenter who helped me reinvent the entire Harmless World with his beautiful covers. Big thanks to my editor Noelle Varner for working overtime to het this one done in time.

And once again, thanks to my readers for always supporting my insane infatuation with Hawaii. And of course to my husband and my girls for their constant support.

JUSTIFIED SECRETS

Everyone has secrets, but hers could get them both killed.

Autumn Bradford has always been a little...different. The daughter of a cult leader, she has spent her life fighting the bad guys and searching for the father everyone thinks is dead. One thing stands in her way, the new leader of Team Bravo.

Former SEAL Seth Harrington accepted the job at TFH for a new start. Years of dangerous missions has left his body and soul scarred. He doesn't have time for a woman with too many secrets and the eating habits of a hobbit-no matter how attractive he finds her.

Autumn doesn't need a keeper or a protector, but every time she turns around, Seth seems to be there. Time together makes it difficult to avoid their attraction, and one stolen kiss makes it impossible to resist the temptation. Falling in love wasn't in the plans for either of them, but Seth realizes he will do anything to protect her, even if it means facing down the most dangerous man either of them know: her father.

Author Note: This is a Harmless World Novel with our

favorite crime fighting heroes and heroines! There are secrets (duh!), inappropriate jokes, Hawaiian food, a betting pool as usual, and a new team to get to know.

PROLOGUE
16 years ago

"Summer," her mother whispered, her voice harsh and full of anxiety. It wasn't anything new. Joseph was a monster. Her mother lived in a constant state of terror. Everyone at the compound did.

"It's time to go."

Summer blinked, trying to get her mind to focus. "What?"

"Let's go. We need to go."

For a long moment, her brain swam in confusion as if it were drowning in denial. Then, finally, something clicked, and she sprang into action. They had planned this for over a month, and it was finally happening.

She grabbed her go-bag and her shoes and ran to join her mother. Silently, they slipped down the hall, their bare feet barely making a noise. They moved like that until they reached the outside of the building. It was cooler outside, a light trade wind dancing over her hair. Fudge, she should have put her hair up. It was too late, but she would fix it when they were free of this cursed compound.

Crowding their bodies up against the outside wall of the house, they made their way to the back of their dwelling. They were lucky that her mother was the only woman legitimately married to Joseph, which afforded them the two-room "house." It was more of a condo with no real kitchen, but it was better than one of the many multifamily units. Those were crowded with people.

Her mother raised her hand. Summer held her breath. The seconds ticked by...the silence surrounding them as fear pounded in her head. She knew it had only been a few seconds, but it felt as if she would die if she didn't take a breath in the next few milliseconds.

Finally, her mother waved her hand. Summer gulped in air as she followed her mother. Their house backed up to the fields, giving them an easy way out if they could avoid the patrols.

Her mother stopped and slipped on her shoes, and Summer followed suit. They hurried to the taller crops that would give them cover as they stole away from Joseph.

They were almost to the edge of their property when the shouts went up, with the sirens sounding. Panic hit her first as they picked up their pace, running and not caring how much noise they made. Their pursuers were getting closer, then they heard the four-wheelers.

Her mother stopped so abruptly that Summer ran into her.

"Oof," Summer said.

Her mother took Summer by her upper arms and propelled her forward.

"Go. There will be a man named Sam Smith. He will take you somewhere safe."

"Where are the other girls, Mama?"

She shook her head, her tired eyes filling with tears. "I couldn't get them out. Just you."

"No!"

"I know you don't think much of me, but you must go.

Sam's an old friend. He knows who you are. Go with him. He will explain everything. Just run straight ahead. He should be waiting on that dirt road back there."

"What does he look like?"

"He's tall, handsome, with dark hair and amber eyes. Go." Her mother pulled her into a hug so tight Summer almost stopped breathing. "Make sure you tell people. We need to save those girls."

Then, her mother turned and cut across the fields, leading the idiots on a chase. Tears filled Summer's eyes. Her mother had just sacrificed herself. Joseph wouldn't hesitate to torture her.

"She's moving North now," Amos yelled out. That guy was a moron.

Knowing that she had to move, or she would end up back on the compound, she turned and ran as fast as she could, knowing those pinheads would pursue her mother and not send scouts out to make sure they hadn't split up.

Her side was hurting by the time she arrived on the dirt road.

"Woah," a cultured English voice said as a man approached her. "Are you okay, love?"

She looked up at the man. Salt and pepper hair, big, strong...and amber eyes.

"What's your name?"

He nodded as if he approved of her question. "Sam Smith. Where's your mother?"

Her eyes filled with tears again. "The guards realized we left too soon. She's distracting them. Can we wait?"

He looked over her head at the fields behind her, the noise of the engines still blaring but further away.

"No. I would like to, love, but Nora made me promise to get you out of here and off the island."

She swallowed the need to argue. One thing everyone at Joyous Wave understood was that arguing could have dire consequences, especially with older men.

"Let's get off this island and then release the news."

"What?"

"Sorry, I thought your mother told you. If she didn't get out of there, I would release the news and let everyone know what has been going on so we can hopefully save your mother and the other girls. But she wanted you off the island."

"They'll see us at the airport."

He smiled a flash of white against the dark Hawaiian night. "Good thing I have my boat. Let's go, Summer."

"I don't want to be called Summer."

He blinked. "Okay, we can talk about that later."

She followed him to the Jeep and climbed in. Within twenty minutes, they arrived at the dock. The boat was a yacht with an entire staff onboard. "Mr. Smith, we're ready to leave as soon as you give us the word."

"Now. We go before any of those bastards can figure out where I took her."

"Yes, sir," he said, hurrying away.

"Come, are you hungry? I ensured there was food here because Nora said you would be hungry."

As if to prove her mother's point, her stomach growled. He smiled. He had a kind one, not calculated, but filled with good humor.

"Who are you?"

He sighed and motioned with his head. "Let's go and grab something to eat. It's a long story."

The moment she stepped into the galley, her eyes bugged out. It was opulent and nicer than anything she had ever seen, but then she'd spent almost every minute of her life at Joyous Wave. While Joseph lived in luxury, the majority of the cult lived in barely standing huts that leaked in rain showers and drowned them in storms.

"Have a seat...wait, what do you want to be called?"

She blinked, then remembered that she had declared she wanted to change her name. "I don't know. I always hated the name, though."

He smiled. "But you were born in the Summer."

She rolled her eyes. "Sounds like a Joseph idea."

His smile faded. "I wish your mother would have called for me. I just didn't know about you, about where she was. I knew she was married to Joseph, but I didn't know."

"You knew my mother before Joseph?"

He nodded as he handed her a glass of water. "I have soda, too."

She'd never had soda before. "My mother?"

"Right. Sorry. You look so much like Nora."

"Are we related?"

"Why do you ask?"

"We have the same eyes. Are you a distant relative to my mother?"

He shook his head. Sadness filled his gaze. "No. But I am related to you, and I will explain everything to you, but let me fix you some food first."

She nodded and looked out the window. Maui grew smaller and smaller into the distance as Sam puttered around the galley. She prayed that her mother would be safe, that she could lie and tell Joseph that she had been chasing Summer. In her heart, though, Summer knew terrible things would happen.

She just didn't know how bad it would be and how many of her friends would die.

Present Day

"Autumn, are you with me?"

Autumn blinked, her gaze focusing on Jin Phillips, soon-to-be Jin Lee. It took her a moment to bring the present back into focus. Jin smiled at her, her kind expression relaxing Autumn's nerves. Not that Jin would have picked up on it. Autumn learned at an early age to hide her emotions.

Her boss's fiancée hosted *Beyond Murder*, a cold case podcast that went beyond just the nitty gritty most true crime shows talked about. As someone who had been the subject of many true crime shows, Jin understood there was more to every story.

Her interest in Autumn came from a case Task Force Hawaii had all worked on a few months earlier. It was then that she had come to Autumn about recording a podcast about her time at Joyous Wave. Autumn had planned on avoiding the subject, but she knew there was one thing that would bring out Joseph: Autumn spilling all his secrets.

"Sorry, I was woolgathering."

"No problem. If you aren't up to talking today, we can handle this another day."

She shook her head. Autumn was usually better at ignoring

the memories, but since Joseph's minions had popped back up a few months ago and wreaked havoc on the island, she'd been falling back into those wretched memories. It had not surprised her that Joseph was entangled in drug smuggling and murders.

"Let's talk about your name change."

Autumn smiled. That was an easy answer. "Rumors were Joseph picked my name."

"And you didn't want any connection to him." Not a question, because Jin researched the people she would interview. "You even went back to your mother's maiden name."

"Officially, I was never a Watters. Joseph wasn't on any of my identification." She shrugged. "Truth?"

Jin nodded. "Always."

"I didn't even have a birth certificate when I ran away from Joyous Wave."

"You mean on you. Was it destroyed in the explosion?"

"I mean, I didn't have one. None. Not that I know of. Nothing was ever filed with the state. I was born on the compound, so there was no official record of my birth."

Jin blinked. "You're kidding me."

She shook her head. "I have no idea why the other kids did. But I was the first born there, so that might be why. Anyway, once I escaped, I had the choice of what name to put on my birth certificate." It had taken her a few weeks to decide, flinching every time someone said her name.

"And you chose another season. Any particular reason?"

"It's the season Sam Smith met my mother. And since he saved me, I thought it was a great way to honor him and my mother."

"Your connection to the Smiths, they adopted you?"

"Yes. Although my brother," she said, using air quotes,

"wasn't thrilled, I totally understood. His mother had just died six months earlier, and here comes this weird girl who didn't know how to operate a computer, let alone how to function in the real world, taking up his father's time."

Another pause from Jin. This is why Autumn rarely talked about Joyous Wave. People were astonished that she had been so backward. "You didn't know anything about computers?"

The old embarrassment threatened to rise up again, but she forced it back. "*Tools of the Devil,* according to Joseph. He used them, but he was the leader, right? I think the entire circle— meaning the stupid men—all had access to them."

"Your education was stunted?"

"That's a nice way of putting it. I was lucky that my mother was teaching me things on the side. Reading for women was allowed, but only scripture."

"The Bible?"

"No, *scripture.* The nut bag had his version of the bible, which was all about him being the Messiah. Want to know a secret?"

"Again, always."

"Joseph was a conman, from start to finish. He never believed he was there to rescue people. He was there to prey upon them."

"Aren't most cult leaders that way?"

"To an extent, but I'm convinced Joseph started Joyous Wave to make money. He was a drug dealer before, during, and after Joyous Wave."

Jin studied her for a long moment. Again, it was the same look she got from almost everyone when she talked about Joseph still being alive. According to the FBI, Joseph Watters was dead.

"So, back to your brother. He's younger?"

"Yes, by about two years."

As if on cue, her phone buzzed on the table. She knew without looking who it was.

> Ian: I said not to do the interview, and you ignored me. WTH?!

She was positive he had some kind of tracker on her or her phone. How did he find things out so fast? It wouldn't be the first time he did it, but it had been years. When she had been undercover as a DEA agent, Ian had been so overprotective. Even as he traipsed the world as a spy for the British government, he somehow kept track of her. After discovering Joseph was back on the islands, he started playing the mother hen again.

"Do you need to take that?"

"No." It buzzed again, and she turned it over. He should know after all these years that he had no control over her. "What else do you want to know?"

She climbed the stairs to her apartment, dreading her showdown with Ian. The moment her foot hit the landing for her floor, two doors opened. Ian stepped out of her apartment, glowering in a way most women would find sexy. She did not.

The other door was Freddy's. His wrinkled face probably came from his time in the sun and the drugs he had taken over the years. The truth was, she had no idea how old he was. Over the last eighteen months, though, she had formed a relationship with him. She paid him for news on the streets about new drugs or dealers.

He smiled at her, showing off his three missing teeth. From his facial features, she knew he was at least a quarter Asian, with dark hair that needed a good wash. He had a scar on his right jaw that looked like it was from a knife. He stood at least three inches shorter than her.

"Hey, pretty Autumn."

"Hey, Freddy. Howzit?"

He frowned. "Not sure."

That was a regular thing. Freddy was still using, and at this point in his life, she wasn't sure he would ever be able to beat the addiction. He had a thing for crack, and it had left his brain mushy. She never knew when she might find him dead, but she knew that day was coming.

"Did you have something for me?"

"Other than that pretty boy giving you the look of death?"

She smiled. Freddy was gay and had a thing for Ian. He talked about her best friend/brother incessantly.

"Yeah, other than that. That I deserve, but don't worry. I know how to handle him."

"I could handle him, too."

She barked out a laugh. "Stop that. You sure you haven't heard anything?"

"Not anything yet, but there's word about a new synthetic on the streets."

She ordered her heart to settle the hell down. There was always something new on the islands, and it didn't mean it was Joseph. The former cult leader loved to deal synthetics, but so did a lot of other bastards.

"Find out where they're selling it, okay?"

He nodded and turned back into his apartment.

"Wait."

Freddy turned around to look at her.

"When was the last time you ate, Freddy?"

"Don't worry about that, pretty Autumn. I'll get you the info as soon as I can."

"No," she stepped forward and dug into her back pocket for a gift card to a local fast-food place. She had them on hand to give to kids on the streets. That way, she knew they would at least get food and not drugs. She held it out and waited. Freddy was the weirdest informant she'd ever had. The man honestly didn't ask for more than he deserved.

"You don't need to give me that."

"I know. But I'll shove it under your door, so save me the trouble and get something to eat."

He hesitated, then took it. "Deduct it from my payment."

"Can't. The money has to be allocated to you, and I would be breaking the law if I did that."

That was a lie. The money Autumn gave him came from her own pocket, but Freddy didn't need to know that.

"Thanks."

He acted like she had given him the most precious gift, and it hurt her heart. People like Freddy were preyed upon by drug dealers and manufacturers. Yes, they were weak to start using. Still, if people like Joseph weren't around manufacturing and selling drugs, they might have found help elsewhere.

She pushed those thoughts aside and turned to head for her apartment. Ian was still glowering at her. Women always lost their heads around him, probably because they didn't know what a pain in the ass he could be. It was the midnight dark hair, blue eyes...and that stupid accent. It irritated her that she couldn't mimic it well. Southern US was about as far as she could get in accents.

"What the bloody hell did you just do?"

"I gave Freddy a gift card for L and L. Are you jealous? I can give you one."

A flush started at his throat and then filled his cheeks. He was her brother, and she loved messing with him. It was fun to watch the former MI-6 agent lose it.

"I'm not talking about that. I'm talking about you being at Jin's."

She rolled her eyes. "No need to get your panties in a twist."

"We talked about this and agreed it was a bad idea."

"First," she said, stepping over the threshold of her apartment, "I didn't agree. You agreed with yourself."

"Dad agreed."

She glanced at him. "Should we call him and check?"

He hesitated.

"That's what I thought. Ian, it's been months since we knew for sure Joseph was back on the island. He hasn't made a move."

She could feel the former cult leader circling her like the shark that he was. He loved head games, so she refused to let him see that it gave her the freaks. By doing the interview, she hoped it would trigger him.

"So you think participating in a podcast that will call him out is a good idea?"

He didn't even try to hide the sarcasm in his voice.

"Do you have another idea? Sitting here waiting for that bastard to make a move is not the smartest thing. That's playing his game."

This argument was tiring her out. Every time they got

together lately, they ended up in a fight about it. She wasn't going to change her mind. This was the only way to draw out that bastard. The only thing she was thankful for was that her brother and father believed her. Most people would nod and ask questions, but there was always a hint of disbelief in their voice that Joseph was still alive.

"And what do you call this?"

"Checkmate."

He sighed. She hated discussing this with Ian. He always took it to heart that she might get hurt. She knew there was a ninety-nine percent chance she wouldn't make it out of this alive. She knew what Joseph was after. The only way he achieved his success was if she were dead. At least if he still believed he was her biological father.

"Did you really tell Dad?"

He shook his head. "He's got enough on his hands right now."

Sam was moving to Hawaii. He'd had a kidney transplant four months ago and decided that life was too short to keep working. With both her and Ian living on Oahu, he picked Honolulu as his new home. It seemed like out of the blue, but Sam was like that. He would brood about something for months before making a decision. The problem was that, in most cases, his actions would put him in harm's way—especially if Ian or she were involved.

"Why is he coming here?"

"You know. He wants to be close to us."

Yeah, she understood that, but there was something else going on with him. Everything had been surface talk lately. He would ask about her job, about the weather...but nothing else. It made her suspicious of his true reason for coming to Hawaii.

Probably because they didn't know her entire plan. And if she worried about it too much, Ian would pick up on it.

"I'm hungry."

"Color me surprised."

Again, sarcasm. Truthfully, she understood it. Her metabolism mimicked a hobbit's. Autumn was convinced that it had to do with her sixteen years in a cult. There was never enough food when she was a kid.

"Let's get something to eat," she said.

"You could cook." One little-known fact about her was her love of cooking. It was something she'd learned after leaving the cult. Since she had to be tutored from home for the first year, she'd spent a lot of time watching TV, which was when she discovered cooking shows.

"Not in that kitchen. It's a death trap."

He followed her out of the door and onto the landing. She locked her door, although she was sure anyone could break in. It's why she rented it.

"I mean at the other place."

She stopped in her tracks and glanced over her shoulder at him. "No. I need to limit my time there now that we know Dear Leader is back on the islands."

He nodded in understanding. She would not lead Joseph there.

"I think I need a big meal."

"You always need a big meal," he said, following her to his car. She was really amazed it still had the tires left. She'd picked this apartment building because it was close to work, and she didn't care if people broke in.

"Where do you want to go?"

She checked the time and realized it was almost six. No

wonder she was hungry. And that meant no Liliha Bakery. Bummer.

"Hmm, not sure. Do we want local cuisine or something else?"

"I don't care, just not a dive bar. I think that last one gave me food poisoning."

"It did not. It was all the alcohol."

He cut her a glance but kept driving.

"I know. Let's hit up that taco place in Aiea. The one in the gas station. Amanda and Felix went there one time, and it looked amazing."

"I need to block that channel."

"Go like you're heading to Bravo's."

"Just for the record, I think you need help with your food fixation," he said as he took the Pali to get on the interstate.

"I don't have a food fixation." She totally did.

"Have you ever noticed that you give directions by restaurant or food truck?"

She frowned. "I do?"

Ian laughed. "Yeah. And why are we going to a gas station to eat?"

"It used to be a gas station, you'll see."

He grumbled but headed in the direction of Aiea. She needed some good food and time with her brother not talking about her childhood.

ABOUT THE AUTHOR

From an early age, USA Today Best-selling author Melissa loved to read. When she discovered the romance genre, she started to listen to the voices in her head. After years of following her AF Major husband around, she is happy to be settled in Northern Virginia surrounded by horses, wineries, and many, many Wegmans.

Keep up with Mel, her releases, and her appearances by subscribing to her <u>NEWSLETTER</u> or join in the fun with her <u>Harmless Addicts</u>!

Check out all her other books, family trees and other info at <u>her website!</u>
<u>If you would want contact Mel, email her at: melissa@ melissaschroeder.net</u>

- instagram.com/melschro
- amazon.com/author/melissa_schroeder
- facebook.com/MelissaSchroederfanpage
- bookbub.com/authors/melissa-schroeder
- goodreads.com/Melissa_Schroeder